DEADHEADING
& OTHER STORIES

Deadheading

& OTHER STORIES

Beth Gilstrap

2019
Red Hen Press
WOMEN'S
PROSE
PRIZE

Red Hen Press | *Pasadena, CA*

Book design by Mark E. Cull

Library of Congress Cataloging-in-Publication Data

Names: Gilstrap, Beth, author.
Title: Deadheading & other stories / Beth Gilstrap.
Other titles: Deadheading and other stories
Description: First edition. | Pasadena, CA : Red Hen Press, [2021]
Identifiers: LCCN 2021014803 (print) | LCCN 2021014804 (ebook) | ISBN
   9781636280004 (trade paperback) | ISBN 9781636280011 (epub)
Subjects: LCGFT: Short stories.
Classification: LCC PS3607.I4556 D43 2021 (print) | LCC PS3607.I4556
   (ebook) | DDC 813/.6—dc23
LC record available at https://lccn.loc.gov/2021014803
LC ebook record available at https://lccn.loc.gov/2021014804

The National Endowment for the Arts, the Los Angeles County Arts Commission, the Ahmanson Foundation, the Dwight Stuart Youth Fund, the Max Factor Family Foundation, the Pasadena Tournament of Roses Foundation, the Pasadena Arts & Culture Commission and the City of Pasadena Cultural Affairs Division, the City of Los Angeles Department of Cultural Affairs, the Audrey & Sydney Irmas Charitable Foundation, the Meta & George Rosenberg Foundation, the Albert and Elaine Borchard Foundation, the Adams Family Foundation, Amazon Literary Partnership, the Sam Francis Foundation, and the Mara W. Breech Foundation partially support Red Hen Press.

First Edition
Published by Red Hen Press
www.redhen.org

Printed in Canada

For Jim and Aubrie

CONTENTS

EARTH EATING AS SUPPRESSION

Up the hill behind Pawpaw's shed, Reese dug in a good bank, pulling handfuls of slippery clay out onto the upturned lid of a garbage can. She squeezed it in her hands, leaving it crimped into mucky dinosaurs. It had rained for a solid week that February and even at her age, she'd learned the best harvests came in winter. Winters in the Carolina Piedmont were like what folks up north call mud season, though we're almost never thawing out frozen. We stay misted and sinking in the ground from November through March. Nobody ever dreamed of a dirty little Christmas, which was almost always what we had. Our trees were trimmed a little more around the bottom after having sat on lots for any amount of time, dirt huddled in the needles, sometimes knee-high. As soon as the carpets and upholstery got cleaned up, the dogs would take one sloppy lap around the property—tongues flying—then come barreling in the doggie door and paint the den crusty red again, the whole time smiling jowly smiles the way only hound dogs could. Pawpaw and Gammie couldn't stay mad for long.

Those dogs were the only thing that made them laugh after a lifetime of scraping by and burying all fifteen of their combined siblings. Both were the last of their families, save for their daughter Verbena and her girl, Reese. They didn't count Reese's daddy no more. Not since he run off with a blonde who wasn't half as pretty or tall or smart as Verbena. They couldn't make heads or tails of it, so they chewed their lips and rubbed their chins and said yes every time they were asked to look after their little tomboy.

Reese had slipped and landed on her knees some time ago, but was so engaged with digging, she'd barely noticed how filthy her new jeans were until the cold soaked in and spread up to her hips. Her fingertips had numbed and her nose prickled in the February air. Daylight waned and the floodlights clicked on, leaving a warm halo to aid her work. Gammie and Pawpaw would holler for her to come in any minute. She wanted to get as much mud as she could before that happened. As her hands stiffened, she rolled a glob in her palms, gently massaging the tender flesh at the base of her thumbs. With one final squeeze, she dropped the last handful on top, wiped the rest on her pant legs because it didn't make no difference anymore, and scooped up the aluminum platter with both hands, as Gammie did any time she served fried chicken to a crowd. Reese's plate was equally special.

Getting up the steps took a ballerina's grace and posture,

but when Reese reached the door, she realized she wouldn't be able to jar the thing loose without a grown-up's help. The house had settled and the ground had shrunk and swollen a million times over between the extreme droughts of summer and the deluge of cooler months. Reese thought a lot about what would happen to her body if she could shrink and swell on the same level of that good red dirt. Would she lizard? Would she water moccasin? Would she worm? She would hole up in a ground nest in summer and lie in wait for a fuzzed creature as soon as she had preened herself free of hair and demands. Pawpaw must've heard her jingling around the door because 'bout the time she'd gotten frustrated enough to throw her mud plate, his haunting silhouette appeared behind the café curtains. He tapped on the glass, asking her if she wanted in.

"Maybe I want to get in of my own accord," Reese said.

"Suit yourself," he said, trying to hide the smile in his voice. But as he stepped away, she changed her mind.

"Pawpaw," she said, no longer fighting balance and full hands and swollen doors. "I got something for you and Gammie."

"Well, then," he said, pulling the door open with a jolt. "I'll take payment upon entry."

Reese walked through the kitchen, where a pot of collards spit and hissed in the pressure cooker and okra cooled on paper towels. Her stomach growled thinking about the cornmeal crunch and the hint of char from the last ones spooned out of the hot grease. On the other side of the kitchen, Gammie was down in the den working a puzzle on a TV tray while the dogs snored next to her. The castle at Magic Kingdom. She had the spires and turrets, but the bottom had yet to be filled in.

"Remember when we met Goofy?" Gammie asked.

"He had the best ears and smelled like ketchup," Reese said, placing her mud plate on top of the puzzle.

"What have we got here? Looks like someone's been up the hill harvesting mud."

"The good stuff," Reese said. "That bit of sour you can't get nowhere but here."

"It's been a long time since I've had a good bit of mud. Folks don't eat it like they used to."

"Only ignorant people partake in such things," Pawpaw said. "Women in particular."

"Don't pay him no mind, baby."

"I didn't have time to make it into pies before supper. It gets dark so early now."

"Come here and sit on my lap and we'll make the patties together."

They sat rolling the mud until it dried in their hands. Gammie told her how her mother salted and baked the clay in the oven and drizzled apple cider vinegar on top, breaking it with her fork while it was still warm. "Some folks won't never understand the desire to let the earth melt under the tongue, to let the thousands of microbes disseminate into the body, to suppress the unnameable pain growing in the belly," she said. "Your mama sure doesn't," she said, raising a piece to Reese's lips and catching the crumbs.

THE DENIAL WEEKS

The dresser got good light in the morning. A sprawling, pooling light that kept the walnut warm. On sunny weekends, I liked to have my coffee in bed. Since the mill was closing soon, I hoped to make it an everyday thing—provided, of course, I could still afford such luxury. But Highland Mill No. 3 wasn't out of business yet, and the calendar said Tuesday, so I figured I'd better get my butt in gear instead of longing for shit I couldn't do nothing about.

As usual, Paul's legs were spread-eagle and his face was still half-covered with the pressed-down-to-nothing wad of a thing he called a pillow. You'd think I'd have gotten sick of looking at this man with his briefs stretched out so much you could see all his business laying there, no covers or nothing, but the strangest things grow on you. Like most mornings, I peeked at him and felt a snicker creep. I couldn't help myself. The truth was, since Daddy died on Mama and the rest of us long before Paul and I are the age we are now, I felt grateful to have good company, if nothing else. I didn't even mind him sleeping in the room next door. We had small rooms and a little space don't do anybody harm. Besides, if he was next to me, I'd never see that sprawled-out something every morning.

I thought money was tight, then. If you'd told me what was coming—that the whole damn structure was about to float away like mimosa tree fluff—I'd have joined my sister at her trailer in Myrtle Beach like she'd asked. But since I wasn't no psychic, I put one foot in front of the other and tried not to let on that the thought of not going to work every day hurt my calves. No matter how much I rubbed them with baby oil or soaked them in Epsom salt baths, the ropes of my muscles had never loosened. It was easier not to look the man in the eye, otherwise I might swing to one of my moods folks don't much care for, the finger-pointer, the crier, the sometimes-violent plate smasher because, damn it all to hell, somebody will share the load, sometime, somewhere. But who was I to complain when I'd agreed to handle the household accounts shortly after we married. Before I took over, we were barely three months into our marriage when Duke Power cut the lights. He confessed he'd bungled it, said he never could make a workable budget, he got sidetracked by shiny things. He said it so cute I'd thought it was a joke, but I learned hell is when a man speaks his truth. But our twentieth anniversary was coming up a week from Tuesday, and there we were, still together, still broke as shit, and losing the jobs we'd never been brave or financially secure enough to walk away from. Still though, I was 80 percent thankful.

"You up?" I asked, cutting off his boxed fan.

He grumbled and rolled to his side, getting twisted in his underwear. "I am now." He shifted himself back into position. "You get the coffee. I'll make us an egg sandwich."

"We're out of bread."

"Got any of those hot dog buns left?"

"Yeah, there's a few. You sure you're up?"

"I'm up. Up, up, up. Glory be it's gonna be one gorgeous day."

"Okay, then," I said, eyes rolling. "I'll start the coffee." The floors creaked down the long hall to the kitchen. The back half of the house was so dark I always wished we'd made enough money to build us a sunroom or have Danny up the street put in a skylight like the one he'd installed for him and his mama. Paul always said if we waited until we had money, we'd be waiting our whole lives and damn if it don't seem like he was right all along. I tried to imagine the kitchen with better light, or what it would have been like if they'd designed the place so the kitchen was where the bedrooms were. It would have made all the difference, but then that was life, wasn't it? Put bedrooms where a kitchen should be and you go through half your life feeling like something ain't right. About the time I sat down and started fantasizing about a supercell storm gifting me hail damage so bad I could have the insurance company remove our dark roof, the doorbell rang.

"Got that, Imogene?"

"You get it. I just sat down."

"I'm trying to find some clean pants. You want me to come up there half-naked?"

"Lord, don't give the rest of creation the view you give me. It's only Earl Jr. anyways."

"What's he want now?"

"I'm fixing to ask him."

The boy stood, waiting for the door to open like he hadn't knocked on it a hundred times in the past year, his eyes startled and half on the verge of tears. Hard not to answer when you know what's on the other side, looking at you like you're the only person who ever offered him a kind word. Boy was so much like a beat dog it wasn't funny, but the state don't take him away because he's more or less fed and clothed, and manages to make it to school most of the time.

"Mrs. Pressley?"

"Come on in, Junior. I'm waiting on the coffeemaker to finish its thing."

"What do you say, Junior? What do you know?" Paul said, buttoning his pants.

"Can y'all give me a ride to school?"

"Miss the bus again?"

"Yeah." He rubbed his nose and brushed his hair behind his ear, but he didn't cry this time.

"Your no-good daddy still drunk?" Paul asked.

"Yeah. Some woman in there with him, too. Saw her uniform on the floor."

"Lord in heaven," I said, pulling a chair out for the boy.

"We'll take you, Junior. Care for an egg sandwich? I'm making me and Imogene one. Got an extra egg anyways."

"Thank you, sir."

"No need to sir me, Junior. We're buds."

We needed that egg for the pancakes I had planned to make for supper, but who was I to say anything? That was Paul. Paul showed him how to fry an egg and as the whites bubbled in the butter, the two of them cut up some—a ten-year-old who seemed twice as old as he was and a man five times his age, but seemed ten, telling knock-knock jokes until they snort-laughed. Paul dangled the spoon on the tip of his nose and for a second, I saw the longing flash across Junior's face. We had to be gentle with this child. Paul didn't understand.

"Hand me them buns, woman."

"Call me that again and I'll hand you something you won't like."

"Okay, okay. Please, Imogene, my love, won't you slide those buns on over here so I can finish making your breakfast?"

"Better. Did you fry mine hard?"

"Yes, love. We cremated the shit out of it, didn't we, Junior?"

"Lord, Paul. Can't you be the grown-up?"

"I've heard worse, Mrs. Pressley."

"I don't doubt that, child. Wrap those sandwiches up. We need to hit the road."

Paul showed the boy how to make "to go" parcels with wax paper so we could eat in the car. He dug two ketchup packets out of the condiment drawer and off we went. In the car, he passed the ketchup to Junior, who dabbed little red circles on his, like ants on a log in some other dimension where everybody makes do all the time. Junior slid the other packet into his back pocket.

"I never had an egg sandwich on a hot dog bun before."

"Us neither," I said. "But whatever works, right?"

"I like the way the egg folded up on itself."

As we turned in the school's main entrance, Junior told us not to pull up front. He didn't want anybody to see who was and wasn't taking him to school. He'd learned a long time ago to lay low. Questions weren't good for anybody.

"Thanks, Paul. Thanks, Mrs. Pressley."

"You're welcome, hon. Have a good day in school." I didn't have the heart to tell him he had ketchup on his T-shirt. Poor kid was always stained.

As we drove away, Paul turned the radio on and sang

along to some old country song I'd never heard. Clouds—the remnants of a gulf-born hurricane—spread themselves thin across the sky, a right nice contrast to the shifting sunlight. It wasn't yet fall, but there was a stray red leaf here and there. I always thought the few weeks before the trees burst into color were the denial weeks. The midlife-crisis weeks. The no-way-are-we-about-to-go-through-the-damn-holidays-and-win-ter-all-over-again weeks. I'd have put money on the fact that those weeks had the highest percentage of extramarital she-nanigans. The last moments of exposed skin before the great seasonal buttoning up and layering and burrowing.

"What's that song?"

"It's a cover of an old Hank Williams song. You wouldn't know it."

"No, I don't guess I would. Since when do you listen to country and western?"

"Dad listened to it when I was a boy."

"I don't recall you ever talking about him and music."

"Do you have to be like this in the morning?"

"Like what?"

"You know."

"I'm only asking questions. Don't make sense is all. Live a lifetime with somebody and he don't mention his daddy liked country and western."

"Hell, hon. It ain't like I set out to keep it from you. It hasn't ever come up."

"You don't talk to me enough."

"Christ, Imogene."

When we got to work, Paul parked in our usual spot under the big maple near the back of the lot. I left the car without saying goodbye and walked on ahead of him so mad I barely paid attention to my feet under me. I tripped over the curb and fell hard on my right knee. Paul came up behind me and helped me up, handing me his handkerchief to dab on the scrape.

"You okay?"

"It's nothing," I said, handing back his blood-spotted handkerchief.

"Why are you passing that back—" He trailed off as he realized the gate was locked and a small piece of paper was taped to the iron above a thick chain. "Posted: Out of Business." It was only after we read the sign that we noticed how few cars were in the lot. Some stragglers came up behind us. Josephine from inspection and Clara from the dye room.

"They could've told us," Josephine said, pulling the scarf off her head and letting the wind muss her hair.

"Maybe they didn't know," Paul said.

"Maybe they did and wanted to get another day's work out of us yesterday."

"Too bad we don't have unions down here," Clara said. "We'd have some kind of recourse. Some kind of compensation."

Josephine said, "Hell, I'd settle for closure. Eighteen years and no goodbye, kiss my ass, or nothing." She pulled a flask out of her hip pocket, took a long pull, and offered us the same.

"Isn't it a bit early?" Clara asked before knocking a little back anyway.

"Who gives a flying fig?" I said. "Give me that thing."

Paul tugged on the gate and looked closer at the sign. "I guess that's that."

"I never thought I would have to deal with finding a new job at my age," Josephine said.

Clara, who was fifteen years our junior, was all optimism and ambition, saying we would all be all right, that this was an opportunity to reinvent ourselves, pursue our dreams, and all that horseshit. Her voice got so amped up and loud, I finally piped in and told her to bring it down a notch. Maybe drink some more of Josephine's cheap vodka. Things weren't the same for us as they were for her. She went on and on about staying friends like losing touch with each other was more harmful than having to go to a damn food bank. But when I saw her a few weeks later at Walmart, her tune had changed. She had a freezer bag full of change, her baby was out of formula and diapers, and her face was beet-red and so sweaty her hair stuck to her cheek. At least I had experience making do.

At first, the opening of our new life was sort of sweet—a

right nice contrast to the never-ending momentum of working days. Paul tooled about in the yard. I lounged and napped and watched game shows and *Little House*. I liked the sway of all that wide, green space, and how nobody seemed cynical even when it all fell to pieces. Smile and pray and believe in the goodness of the human heart. We ate rice and beans for dinner the first week. For our anniversary, Paul wanted to try to do something special so I sold some clothes that didn't fit anymore and bought generic brand cold cuts and sliced cheese, spicy brown mustard, and mayonnaise. We made sandwiches and packed some of that fake lemonade that comes in a gallon jug.

"Seems like a good day to go to the lake," he said, pouring ice in the cooler. When he was happy with the ratio of ice to food, he put a trash bag over top of it as extra insurance the sandwiches wouldn't get wet and soggy. The man hated soggy more than you'd think possible.

"Probably the last warm day for a stretch. Supposed to turn cooler tomorrow."

"I can't believe it's been twenty years," he said, kissing me on my bare shoulder and opening the truck door for me. I swore I would put the bills and the constant puzzle-working anxiety that comes from being broke out of my head for the afternoon. Focus on us. Toast a lengthy marriage. If things had continued like that the rest of the day, we might have made it even longer. But that's not the way of things. Just ask Clara.

We rolled the windows down. With warm air whipping my hair around, I felt like a girl again. At a stoplight where two sides of the crossroads were planted down with tobacco and the other two with cotton, Paul said, "Turn around for me." He took a rubber band off the gear shift, brushing my hair with his fingers the best he could, separating it into three sections for a braid. With his hands looping my hair so close to the back of my neck, I closed my eyes and breathed in the grassy smell of the country. Before he had the braid fastened, a semi pulled the horn on his rig, knocking us out of our bewilderment.

"I can get it the rest of the way," I said. "Better get to it before the jackass behind us has a conniption."

When we got down the road a ways, the excitement had waned. We were still the same unemployed, middle-aged couple who slept in separate rooms. The truth was that both of us were terrified and had no intention of talking about it. Paul still tried to engage me by reminiscing about our courtship—how he'd first seen me in town with my mama, pulling a red wagon full of groceries behind us, how if he'd judged by how I fit into my yellow dress, he'd have never known how poor we all were—but it still didn't take me long to give up on my happy mood altogether. When I put my face in the wind, he quit, too. Maybe I could live there

in the movement of air over a vehicle that had taken us up and down the East Coast. I could cease having to pay for things, having to work, having to keep trying to fix every damn thing in my tiny world.

About that time, the truck sputtered a time or two and rolled to a stop.

"Well, that's that," Paul said.

"What's wrong now?"

"Out of gas."

"Figures," I said. "I guess you didn't feel the need to warn me."

"I hoped we'd make it."

"And what was the plan for getting home?"

"I thought we could borrow some gas from somebody up at the lake."

"Lord in heaven. What a plan."

"We could still have a day together," he said, pulling the keys out of the ignition. "Come on, Imogene. We're only about a mile from the lake. I'll carry the cooler. You get the blanket. We'll deal with this later. It ain't going anywhere

"Fine," I said. "But when it comes time, you're the who's got to go beg strangers for gas." I slid my flip-back on and draped the blanket over the top of my to He fiddled with the cooler, muttering somethin how the drive must've been bumpier than he rea

careful packing of the cooler hadn't held up as much as he hoped it would; it didn't stay as cold as it should've.

"It's the consistency of your failed hopes and wishes and all your big, whirlybird dreams that gets me."

"That's right. Make it bigger than it need be."

"You're the one whining about your cooler not being cool enough." I caught it that time—the cruelty welling up in me for no good reason so I tried to soften, to put a silk filter between my meanness and Paul. "I'm sorry, babe," I said, slowing my gait enough to walk side by side. "Don't make sense. Nary a cold cut should have budged."

He said thank you but I could tell by the way he watched his feet as we walked that my demeanor had taken its toll. I wished more than anything I could go back to the moment he pulled over and tell him to forget about the rig behind us, let the driver have his conniption so long as he finished my braid, pulled my back to his chest, and slapped the fat of both thighs like we were nineteen again. I wished I could shore up gratitude for having had him in my life all those years, but it was hard to be grateful when collectors rang your phone twenty times a day and your husband came in joyful from a day of mowing lawns up and down the block, barely bothered by the growing space between items in your kitchen cabinets.

We walked on—up the last hill before the lake and down into the curve leading to the trail. This particular

access point had been around since our parents' generation though it had all but grown over. We avoided the new public beach for fear of crowds even on a weekday. It had been years since we'd been there ourselves. Paul walked ahead, using the cooler to push through the brush, holding back branches for me to pass. The lemon-sweet scent of decaying magnolia leaves warmed my temper a little.

As luck would have it, the spot was empty and the old diving board still floated on a small dock about twenty yards from shore. I spread the blanket out directly in front of it so if you came upon the scene it would be like some Italian movie man had planned it out, with the gentle lap of the water a foot from our cooler, the clear yellow of it a right nice contrast to the avocado cotton. Paul sighed, content.

"I don't know about you," I said, sliding the lid off the cooler. "But I'm starving."

"I could eat."

I started making our plates, but something was wrong. I counted one bologna and two turkey sandwiches. "Someone's been in this thing."

"I knew it," he said, crawling over on his hands and knees. "Let me see."

"The lemonade ain't here and we're missing a bologna sandwich."

"If that don't beat all. When could someone have gotten in there? When we were stopped at that crossroads?"

"I don't think we were there long enough, Paul. You didn't even have enough time to finish my hair."

"But it's so strange. It don't feel right."

"It's just bologna and lemonade. Or rather, lemon drink. Let's eat so we can swim. We wasted a lot of daylight on the drive up."

"But—"

"But nothing. Don't you reckon anyone who was hard up enough to take bologna might as well be left alone? I'm trying here."

"Okay, okay. You can have two. I'll be fine with one."

I pulled the damn thing in two, handing him half.

"Thank you," he said with a hint of shame.

In between mouthfuls of white bread and poor quality meat, we tried to remember every time we had gone swimming together in the past twenty years. It was a sweet exercise filled with limb-entwined memories of pontoon boats and freckles, of cliffside leaps, salt spray, and bathing suits lost in the surf, of our black lab Dolly swimming out to the dock now in our eyeline again. It was peculiar to recall the temperature variations from all those bodies of water we'd waded in, but the strangest things occur to you when you start comparing all the thousand times you've experienced one thing. The thousand times I've walked past Paul in the morning. The thousand ways his face and mine have changed. The ten thousand ways I've put off this bill for that.

The way it's all basically the same except for little details like the coolness of the water. Drowsiness set in and before my mind had a chance to turn again, I stood up, holding out both hands to Paul. "Let's go," I said. And so, we swam out to the diving board.

Pushing ourselves up was more difficult than it used to be, but we managed with only a few knee-cracks and shoulder spasms. "Who's first?" he asked.

"Go ahead. I need to catch my breath."

He was careful in his ascent, keeping both hands on the rails. Once atop, he bounced, but hesitated long enough to shield his eyes from the sun. "Someone's out there," he said. "And he seems to be headed straight for our stuff."

"What should we do?"

"Hell, Imogene. Can't say as I know."

"Go on and jump. We can't get there before he takes anything, if that's what he wants."

"I suppose that's true," he said, without taking his eyes from shore.

His bounce turned to a quick jump and he dove without flourish.

When he resurfaced, he blew water from his nose. "That hurt worse than I remember. Your turn."

"Maybe I shouldn't."

"You'll be okay. I'm here."

I'd like to say I was graceful, but the way I hit the water

would purple my right side for a month. But Paul told the truth—he was there. He helped me get back by wrapping my arms around his neck and dog paddling toward shore. Once we reached shallow water, he yelled for the person rummaging in our cooler. Paul was more surprised to see it was Junior than I was.

"Junior, if there's any ice left, bag it up so we can put it on Mrs. Pressley's ribs."

"It's all melted."

"You took our sandwich?"

"Yeah."

"What are—how did—"

"I thought if I could sneak out here with y'all, maybe I could get away for good."

"You're running away?" I asked.

"Never mind," Paul said. "We're glad you're here. Let's pour some of that cool water in the garbage bag. You hold it open, Junior."

He held the bag as wide as he could, but Paul's pour was off and most of the water hit the ground, me, and the blanket. "You couldn't have done that away from the blanket?"

"Oh God, I'm sorry. I'm so sorry." He held the bag and its piddling contents, unsure of what to do next.

"Can't we put lake water in the bag?"

"It's too warm."

"Call off the cavalry," I said. "Give me a little while to adjust to the pain, then we'll pack up and start trying to find our way home." Junior flinched at the idea of going home. It took half an hour or more, but the two of them finally calmed down enough when Junior mentioned a scouting mission for medical supplies. I lay there on the hard ground, drying out and wishing (for the thousandth time) I could do it all different. Every last thing.

They returned with a walking stick and informed me that they would be wrapping my torso with the blanket. I looked ridiculous, but I had to admit once they finished spooling the thing around me it did offer some relief. It took more than an hour for us to reach the road. Paul and Junior stuck their thumbs out, hopeful and drunk on adventure.

"You're kidding. This is your plan?"

"No choice."

And as I propped myself up on the stick, trying to maintain balance so I didn't wind up like a turtle on my back, I knew they were right. A family in a VW bus stopped for us right before dusk. The two kids climbed to the back row, letting the weirdos from the street, as they referred to us, have the middle.

"Thank you for giving us a ride," I said.

They asked what had happened and told us they were driving their kids across the country. They'd been driving for weeks. The youngsters might not appreciate the scenery and wildlife and road time now, but they would one day.

"I'm not so sure," the woman said, catching my eyes in the rearview. "You know what I mean?"

She had the look of a woman who'd been cooped up for too long. She wiped sweat from her neck with a handkerchief. This was a woman who'd rather leave the kids with her parents, jet off to Paris, and sit for portraits. She was too thin-boned and lipsticked to have packed trail mix and car games, to sing songs with the family, or eat burnt hot dogs on sticks. I felt like she could disintegrate gazing at her own reflection. It didn't take her long to turn away when she realized the boy must not be mine. The coloring was off. Bone structure, too.

Junior lay his head on my lap as best he could. I had more heft than usual thanks to the blanket. I petted his head, rapt by the texture of his forehead, his hair. It took the better part of the ride, but eventually he closed his eyes and drifted off. It wasn't all I would lose in the coming months that got me. Not the big armchairs. Not the thousand tulip bulbs I'd planted over a lifetime. Not the sunken den we added on in the boom years. Not even the comfort of Paul splayed out on his bed. It was the sight of Junior's face softened by sleep that made the inevitable move more than I could bear.

BONE WORDS

The grass marks on his cheek when he rolled over kept me from waking him. A clump of clippings at his zygomatic bone. God knows what burrowing near his neck, near the occipital bone, along the base of his skull, where I'd held him. Soft spots no one thinks on. I like paying attention to places on a body most people take for granted. A smear of my lipstick (color, Medieval) true to its claim, everlasting on his Adam's apple—that sweet hunk of thyroid cartilage named for sin. His eyes, hair falling across them, still closed, still twitching like the horned beetle I'd picked off the dead pine next to our tent. I'd read in biology how when you see them, rarely anytime but dusk, they're only ever searching for their lovers or fighting—other males, only males, of course always fighting—for decaying fruit or sap, favored mating grounds close to rotten wood. The sleeping boy is too sweet for fighting. He writes songs about my hair. The sleeping boy's brother will find out about us alone in the old growth, our chapped skin, our damaged tent, and helplessly hope our similar smells are his imagination gone dark. I found no female, but the beetle's hiss and mandible impressed me, a dribble of my own saliva hanging as I petted his head, fighting the urge to tie a string around his dorsal plate and wear him as an amulet. Later, I will want to tell the sleeping boy's brother how lizards and snakes and beetles of the family *Lucanidae* have vast variations in size between juvenility and adulthood, how their bodies are bound to environment with only a smidge of genetic influence, but all I can explain before he slams the door is how females have smaller, more powerful jaws. When I drive away, I will say "mandible" out loud to an empty car and roll all the windows down, praying for rain, praying for wings, praying for horns of my own.

A FIVE-POINTED,
FAILED PAPER LOVE WEAPON

You wear your hair down and your brother's jeans the day the only boy you date freshman year staples himself in the chest. You are still sticky from gym because you can never bring yourself to shower in front of people, but you hope the perfume you stole masks the odor. You blot your cheeks, nose, and chin before you see him on the path to yearbook. He's everything your girlfriends told you to want. Black hair hanging over one eye. Patches on a moto jacket. Tight-rolled jeans. Messed up like you.

You try to speak to the boy, to tell him you want to take his boots home to your room to eat, to put your forefinger on his eyelids and absorb the image you know can't be unseen, the one of his friend hanging by a chain from a dogwood, to tell him how the gravel sound of his voice makes something in your hip bones crack, how the pain in your chest at night after he finally hangs up must make you the youngest person in the world who suffers heart attacks. But all you can do is touch his skull earring, ask where he got it.

As he leans you up against the locker, you notice the dust

mop smell of the hallway, doors clicking closed, and a few straggling runners trying to make it to class. You are late. You squirm away and dig a knuckle into your sternum. He pulls his own hair.

"Fine. Whatever. I thought you loved me."

You try to give him the love letter you folded into a star, but he flicks your arm away, sending it sailing to the floor—a failed paper love weapon you lift off the linoleum by two of its five points. In yearbook, you cut pictures and wax them onto mockup pages. Candid shots of Emily and Allison and Farrah all branded-up like race car drivers and lording over each other. No one's permission ever given or granted to separate. An image of the math nerds lined up eating bag lunches on the floor at the back of the cafeteria. The full-page in memoriam for his friend's suicide his parents said was an accident. You snip your open palm and watch your own blood bead. When you see him again after school, he is halfway to his car. You run, your backpack thumping so hard it hurts your shoulders.

Wait for me, the girl who knows how to bruise herself.

He turns after he unlocks his car door. On the white lettering of his Black Flag T-shirt, red spots soak through, spaced the width of staples. Seventeen staples equal thirty-four holes. You ask what's wrong. He says "you don't love me" so many times the words become nothing but moan. You reach in through the window, touch his knee, and take a cigarette from the dash, leaning over him to light it. You take a drag and lean back against his car door. Without looking back at him, you smoke your cigarette like you have nothing else to do. The Emilys and Farrahs are waiting. When you finish, he passes you an empty Coke can for the butt and tells you to get in the car. Before he drops you home, he pulls off into an adjacent field. Amid swaying weeds and broken bottles, you kiss all thirty-four of his wounds, wishing he were the first or the last violent man in your life.

NO MATTER HOW FINE

Janine worked longer hours than most women her age, but she wasn't quite ready to admit it was all for naught, that her shop was failing. In the quiet after closing, when she shut the music off and she sent her employees home, the lines in her forehead softened. Her shoulders fell into their natural slope, and she came back to the parts of herself she kept closed off to everyone except her father and Maddie. It was summer and she loved how the shadows lengthened and dappled, leaving the red sofa in a romantic haze. The track lighting she'd invested in could never do that. If she could've harvested those soft edges all year, maybe she would've sold more furniture. But how much can lighting possibly matter when everyone's upside down on their houses and can't afford gas? Still, Janine loved her store. The till caught a glare so she moved the paperwork to the farmhouse table next to the register. The table had a long scratch down the middle and its legs were cracked from too many shifts in moisture and heat, but rustic was popular thanks to those yahoos on HGTV. She crouched over, counting bills into straight piles.

Six twenties. Five tens. Four fives. And twenty-seven ones. Tapping the pile on the table, she straightened it into a neat brick and looked up, squinting. On these days when sunlight appeared almost watered down, Janine always thought of her grandma. She zipped the deposit bag, reached to the light board behind her, and flipped black switches to the off position, four at a time. Her store darkened like a stage. Section by section. Sofa by sofa.

Her grandma would tell her to do something about the extra inventory. No matter how fine the furnishings, crowding made everything in a room seem like junk.

The shop Janine opened was a life-sized shadow box less than a mile from where her grandma had lived most of her life, where the ranch houses gave way to a lane of glass storefronts. This was Midwood. A neighborhood that used to be populated by former G.I.s and their families now housed their widows interspersed with twenty-year-olds who wore artistic mindsets and tight jeans. Trees had been planted along the main plaza in the late forties; now, their branches touched, making the street a cove. Janine loved this about Charlotte—its green fortress created by willow oaks. Some people remarked on their beauty and thanked the Lord for shade. And some folks hated them because of the pollen that built up like snowdrifts come March and April. Wealthier families wrapped their trees with black belts to protect them from a particularly dangerous breed of beetle, but Janine hadn't grown up on that side of town. She grew up closer to Eastland Mall with her father, where the trees were still staked down, where owners tried to keep them from growing crooked or falling. Where the houses were four models repeated over and over down every street.

Before opening day three years ago, Janine had her dad and Maddie help unload the first truck. Janine checked off numbers on her clipboard, signed her first vendor invoice, and slapped the driver on the shoulder, giddy from possibility, her hair frizzing in the humidity of a summer morning. But by late afternoon, her dad had strained something in his groin. Janine could tell by the way he tucked his back when he walked, but he didn't say a word. He told Janine when he leaned in to kiss her on the forehead that her grandma would be proud.

"I can see her now, clad in a pantsuit, one of those Styrofoam cups in her hand, shuffling through here, nodding. She'd like the white sofa. Probably that wild disco lamp too," he said, tying his blue bandana on his head.

"You really think she'd like it?"

When she retired from Highland Park Mill, her grandma kept on sewing. She made the slipcovers on her furniture along with Janine's clothes. Jumpers and smocked dresses. On their mall trips, her grandma would wobble and grab at Janine's hand. From behind, she resembled a shopping rhinoceros, and with great snorty breaths, she'd situate plastic bags in the crook of her elbow and balance Orange Julius cups under her chin. The sight of her was magic.

"I do think she'd like it. Mama always could make a house shine, just like you," he said. "Except the ceiling. She'd say it looked like the mill. Too exposed. But you'll get to that when you start selling some of this junk. This neighborhood should love it. This fake old shit. You'll have those old big-hairs in here in no time, stinking up the place with that Chanel garbage your mother used to wear."

"God, I hope so. I need big-hairs all over the place. I don't care if they're doused in kerosene. Send them over. Too bad you don't have any friends to push my way," she said, twisting again under the weight of impractical clothes. She'd change into the spare jeans she kept in the trunk of her Honda after he left. "Besides, I'm going to bring in authentic vintage, too, Dad. I have a few pieces at home I got from an estate sale. A walnut vanity and a settee. Speaking of." Janine put her clipboard down on the asphalt, put her hands together, and stuck out her lip—a trick that never failed to work on her father.

"Next Saturday work?" he asked, rubbing his elbows. "I have some side jobs coming up this week so I can't do it until the weekend. And, darlin', what in God's name is a 'settee'?"

She sat down on the curb, kicked her shoes off, and patted the sidewalk. "It's like a love seat, Dad, but fancier, I guess."

"Honey, if I get down there, I ain't ever getting up," he said. "My knees."

"I'm working you too hard."

"Nonsense. I can't crawl around on the ground as well as I used to."

About that time, the trash truck squeezed through the thin lane behind Cotswold Shopping Center, backing up next to her dad's truck, hissing and beeping.

"I hope he stays clear of my baby. She's paid for and I'd hate to see her dinged."

The truck's cobalt patina had faded long ago, but the white wall tires shone. The letters had peeled off, leaving the F-O-R-D a darker shade of blue. A dolly was strapped to the back and a Gandalf action figure hung from the rear-view mirror. For Janine, that truck was an extension of her dad. She couldn't imagine him driving anything else. That truck was part of the landscape. Part of his home. It had left permanent grease stains on the asphalt in front of the house. Her memory lay in the bed of that pickup. Summer days when the metal burned her bare legs and feet. Even when she got tired of the old neighborhood and the whole of Charlotte, Janine never thought of trying to live any other place.

But Janine's dad didn't have much of a poker face when it came to where he grew up. She knew he was disappointed she hadn't gone away to school, but she loved how he tried to be positive about the store for her sake, though he wasn't always successful. He'd always said he felt suffocated by so much consistency. The same front porches with the same two concrete steps. Some would paint them green or dark gray. His mother had painted the whole porch white and put down a piece of outdoor carpet, not unlike AstroTurf. He'd rolled matchbox cars over the high grass and sent them shooting over the edge of the cliff into the azaleas—the same shrubs that were planted in front of every porch, mocking him with hot pink flowers he'd rip off as he walked past. Her grandma had sat on that porch, cross-stitching, smushing cigarette after cigarette into a crystal ashtray, somehow managing not to burn the fabric. Janine had sat on that porch, bickering with him about his ideas on uniformity until he'd concede Janine was different. Her shop was different.

"Okay, then. I'll help you with your so-called settee. Shit," he said, "why can't people call stuff by what it is? And what, no tête-à-têtes?" he asked, poking her in the kidney. He dug his keys from his pocket.

"Could you stop being so you? For today."

The man was tickled and laughed all the way to his truck, limp and all.

"Love ya," he said over his shoulder.

"You too."

Maddie came through the back door, her arms full of

fabric samples. "Where do you want these? Do we have hangers? Where's he off to, anyway? I thought he was going to stay and help unpack all this shit," she said, struggling to hold on to the load of blue and green fabric squares. "I dropped half these things on the way out."

"He's hurt himself," Janine said, scooping half the stack from Maddie's arms. "Looks like it's just the girls."

"ABC store's across the parking lot."

"Maybe after we get the store set up. I worry about Daddy," she said, as she and Maddie set the fabric on the sidewalk. They walked to the Honda together. "Something's off."

Janine's dad had told her he'd only stayed in this town for her mother, a woman whom he'd loved for her Kiss T-shirts and wall of hair. Said she'd hooked him from the start with promises and gumption. "Not for her, I'd a up and left when I was eighteen," he'd always said.

Her mother had left them on Janine's seventh birthday. Janine heard it over and over but chose not to listen anymore how her dad would've done this, that, and the other if only he could've gotten away. The truth was her daddy saw himself as more of an *Easy Rider* type than he turned out to be. Janine's never known him to wander, even through town. Maybe that's why her mom left—because of routine. Most days he was so worn down, he sat on his porch in an Adirondack chair, four Budweisers beside him. Exactly four. Knew his limits. Been doing that since he and Janine's mother had moved back to the neighborhood and closer to Janine's grandparents. Now, he was stuck in their old house. He had moved in and sold the house he had shared with Janine and her mother when his father took sick. Obligation will fall like a blackout curtain if you let it.

The truck sputtered. He hung his arm out the window, banged on the door, and then waved goodbye as he drove off.

As she watched the truck, she wondered if he was right about her grandma. She liked to think they were working on this place together, partners in crime beyond the grave. When Janine was young, they spent many days together—gathering goods and making plans for all the things they were going to make, but Janine could feel the desperation in it, even at that age; she knew it was all to keep from sitting still. The two, separated by a generation of guilt, had that in common. It wasn't any surprise when she opened a shop some twenty years after her grandma passed, after the last time she sat at her knee, holding the bolts of fabric up from the floor so she could watch her grandma cut them with toothy pinking shears. Janine rescued remnants, especially the silks, and even now, if a silk was discontinued, she'd take the swatch home.

"He's fine, Janine. He's getting up there," Maddie said, waiting for Janine to open the trunk. "I can't believe you got dressed up for today. What the hell?"

"I don't know. I wanted to look the part, I guess. But I

didn't think about dirty cardboard and picks in my hose. I blame the hour. Keep an eye out," she said, slipping into the backseat and pulling off her skirt and hose. The jeans came up soft.

"Better?"

"Better," Janine said, leaving her skirt and hose folded into a square on the back seat.

"Let's do this," Maddie said, reaching out and pulling Janine up from the car. They stretched, arms up and wide.

Janine looked at Maddie, her exposed belly. "Plaza Midwood—hell all of Charlotte—better love my store or my fat ass will be camped at my grandparents' house with Dad in a year."

"That happens, I'll help you set up your tent."

Janine and Maddie stayed until 3:00 a.m. cutting the plastic off sofas, screwing the legs on tables, and playing house. When they finished vacuuming and wiping shelves down, Maddie got out her cigarette holder and fastened a Camel to the end.

"I'd really prefer you not smoke in here."

"Just this once. You don't open for a couple days. We'll open the doors tomorrow." They stretched out on chaise lounges and talked in their best Katharine Hepburn voices, jutting their chins and arching their backs.

"You know why I like her?" Maddie asked.

"The cheekbones?"

"Because she wore men's slacks and didn't believe in Jesus." Maddie had that way about her, saying things people never expected, and it was more pronounced by her wide-set eyes.

"I don't know about that."

"No, I read it in a book about famous atheists."

"You read something?"

"Suck it. I read."

"Your mother would be so proud," Janine said, smacking her head on a table.

"At least I don't need a helmet," she said, getting up to pay the delivery man. "I'm taking a twenty from your wallet." By the time Maddie walked back with the food, their laughter had quieted but not to awkwardness. They'd known each other most of their lives. Maddie knew when to distract Janine and when to let the mood shift. They ate pizza on the floor and drank soda from paper cones, content in each other's company.

Three years later, Janine struggled to keep the store open. Every night she counted fewer bills in the drawer. That night as she locked the door, she saw a silver sedan at the end of the parking lot. She put her keys in between her fingers and walked to her car. She could see someone's silhouette, but her eyes weren't so great at night, particularly when she forgot her glasses. She got in, locked the doors, and, to be safe, drove to her grandparents' old house, where her dad now lived.

"Daddy? You up?" she asked, as she walked in the back door. He sat rocking back and forth in the glider, watching *Hogan's Heroes*. The glider was one of the few pieces he'd brought from their old house. Most of it he'd taken to Goodwill. He hadn't made it his home.

"I'm up," he said.

"Can I stay here tonight? There was some creep watching me outside the store."

"Sure, babycakes," he said, never taking his eyes off the screen. "There's chili in the fridge if you're hungry."

"Babycakes? You drunk, old man?"

"Maybe a little."

"Figures. You save me some?"

Janine heated up a bowl of chili, cracked a can of Budweiser, and wondered how this house still managed to smell like her grandmother all these years after her death. Maybe she had smelled like the house. Like talcum and Chanel and cigarette smoke. The white café curtains her grandma made, yellowed from countless Virginia Slims lit and burned so many years ago? No one would replace them.

When she got back to the den, her dad was asleep with his mouth open. She took the remote from his hand, covered him with the red and black afghan, and switched it to *The Daily Show*. She thought if this house was ever hers, she'd paint the paneling, get rid of that midcentury look.

He snored himself awake.

"What's this about someone watching you?"

"I don't know. There was some silver car at the end of the lot with no lights on, just sitting," she said, scraping the bowl.

"You carry that stun gun I gave you?"

"No, I left it at home."

"Maybe I should teach you to shoot," he said, raising an eyebrow at Jon Stewart's Jersey guy accent. "Funny. Who is this guy?"

"You never watched Jon Stewart?"

"No, hon, I ain't." He stood. "You want to go to the range tomorrow?"

"You know I don't believe in guns."

"Said the woman who got so spooked she came to spend the night with her dad."

"I gotta be at the store early. You turning in?"

"I reckon so," he said, rocking himself out of the recliner.

"Wanna get breakfast in the morning?"

"I'll make you waffles," he said, mussing her hair. "Long as you don't care if they're Eggo."

"Can't wait," she said.

As he creaked his way up the steps, she put her bowl in the sink and filled it with water. She walked through the kitchen into the dining room, touching the pea-green wallpaper. The mirror reflected light from the street lamp because her dad never bothered to pull the lace curtains closed, said anybody who wanted to see him was free to watch. She walked over to the window, blew on it, and made a baby footprint with the fleshy part of her fist. She thought she saw the tail end of the silver car as it passed, but when she lay her forehead against the window, she could only make out taillights.

She wondered about her dad, how he slept these days, whether his back was any better. She meant to ask him. She always meant to. A man walked by with a basset hound. She thought of Applejack, her grandma's old mutt who used to always knock his head on the table legs. She used to play with him and feed him broccoli when no one was looking. She got down on her knees. The blue bubblegum wad was still there, spread wide and thin. Tomorrow, over Eggos, she would ask her dad if she could have the table for the store. She knew he'd say yes.

She took a deep breath and walked to the next room over, the little room, her grandma used to call it. It was a guest room and her grandma's sewing room all in one. A single bed was pushed against the window. The pillows her grandma had cross-stitched still sat arranged in the same order. Cardinals on the left, the little girl kneeling and praying—*Now I lay me down to sleep*—in the middle, and violets on the end.

As a child, she had stared out the window at the street-light and wondered what her life would be like, if her mother was looking at the same stars, if she thought of her. She'd sleep with all the pillows on the bed and get upset whenever they fell on the floor. When she couldn't sleep, Janine would trace the raised stitches, think of the looped packages of thread, the yellow plastic box with removable trays her grandma kept them in, the old butter mint tin she kept her buttons in, how she'd dump them on the floor and try to find matches. Her grandma let her play with all her sewing stuff, but she never let her work the machine on her own. After she died, Janine took the box of thread and the button tin home with her. She never had the heart to learn to sew for real but every now and then she'd cross-stitch a Christmas ornament, something simple with only X's. She'd have to tape up the back of them because she never learned the proper way to finish a piece.

The sewing machine still had its plastic cover on. A tomato pincushion sat next to it. Reds, yellows, and blues clustered together in tiny balls of color. Janine ran her fingers over the pins. She pushed them all down completely. She'd take this, too.

Janine pulled out her grandma's ladder-back chair, retied the strings of the cushion, and took a seat. Someone had dusted recently. She pulled the cover off the machine. It was cream and sage green. A sixties Singer her grandma would never have parted with. There was still a spool of thread in the top, half-used. She always wondered what her grandma had been working on when she died. She turned the hand-wheel. The needle moved.

Her grandma had kept the patterns in a filing cabinet next to the machine. It'd been years since Janine touched the collection. She liked the sketches on the outside. The women were always trim and made-up with architectural hair. They struck poses with their hands held out to their sides, looked like they'd just turned around, caught in a moment of glee that could only be caused by a great pair of pleated trousers or a tea-length dress worn with white gloves. As she rummaged, she found the patterns for a lot of her own childhood clothes. The overalls her grandma had sewn in red corduroy were there represented in denim. All her Christmas and Easter dresses. She wondered what her grandma would've made her as an adult. A white pantsuit? A simple A-line dress. Indigo. Soft pink. Butter yellow.

When Janine realized she didn't have anything to sleep in, she walked upstairs, using her phone as a flashlight so she wouldn't disturb her father. He slept in his boyhood room since he'd moved back in. Hadn't had the nerve to take over his parents' room. She crept down the hallway past his cracked door to her grandparents' old room. She knew her dad hadn't been able to part with her grandpa's clothes yet.

She pulled out a plain white T-shirt, wondering if it was creepy to sleep in the clothes of the dead.

It felt cool as she pulled it over her head, smelled like cedar. She looked over at their full-size bed and the eaves on the right side of the room. Her grandma slept on that side of the bed because she was a good head shorter than her grandpa. She remembered the long gowns her grandma had slept in and how her grandpa slept outside the covers in nothing but his birthday suit. Her grandpa had gotten rid of her grandma's clothes, even the ones she'd made. Said he couldn't take looking at them anymore. Janine had told him she'd take them but he'd told her, "Girl, that ain't natural. You gotta get on with your life."

Her grandpa's shirt hit her midthigh. Standing in the doorway to their room, she flipped the switch and hugged her own clothes to her chest, feeling palpitations. She closed her eyes, breathing in the smell of the furnace being turned on for the first time in months. Grandma Sue was there in her poppy housecoat with red pockets, telling her to turn in, settle down, that she'd be down in a few to tuck her in.

Back in the little room, Janine rolled into a ball under the covers. In the blue-tinted light of the street lamp, she strained to remember the feel of her grandmother's hand on her head.

SALE DAY

In line for coffee, Janine chewed the callus on her thumb and watched a baby gum the top of a chair, her fat legs buckling. The mother patted the baby's butt and Janine wondered if she'd ever get a chance to do such a thing. Pressed against strangers, she dove into images of a woman with Linda's body mashed with Celia's face, round with the traits of pregnancy, but she didn't stay in that place long. It was a muddle of blonde memory and hopeless fantasy and this was sale day. She had to focus. Twelve hours to make it or break it. The baby wiggled in her yellow corduroy overalls, looked at Janine, chair still in her mouth, and let out a squeak. Janine imagined the feel of the girl's tender gums pressing against the cool metal and took her own thumb out of her mouth.

Furniture polished. Carpets shampooed. She hoped the bathrooms wouldn't see too much activity. The plumbing was delicate and it wouldn't do to have the pipes back up today. The store had to be perfect. When the weather warmed, people freshened up their homes and Janine needed the day to go well. The recession had left her on a hinge that could swing toward bankruptcy any day. Her glasses were too loose, her jeans thinning. Objects aged. If the store could be cleared of most of the old merchandise, she could start over with brighter colors—the turquoise she'd seen at market, jaunty florals, pink hibiscus on Tar Heel blue. Lemon-colored melamine chairs. A light fixture like an upside-down money tree, luminescent above a mahogany dining table. She had thought about hiring people to stand at the intersection with signs, but she wanted to keep the whole thing sophisticated, hated red-faced guys who yelled *Sundy, Sundy, Sundy* into cameras. Hated their ill-fitting suits. Their awful drawls. She wasn't some hick. She was cottage. Boutique.

On the ten-mile drive to work, Janine took in the landscape through a dirty windshield, its overgrown quiet on Saturday morning, the abandoned dealerships and head shops on Independence Boulevard whose last rites had come in the form of a bypass. She passed the spot in front of the Exxon station where her grandmother was T-boned turning left. She kissed her fingertips and held them to the window.

Going the back way, Janine saw signs of squatters—mattresses at the back of the boarded-up Family Dollar, graffiti, candles in mason jars that made her think of *Emmet Otter's Jug-Band Christmas*. Grocery carts littered the parking lot, and the old home-cooking joint where she'd eaten countless plates of grits and eggs with her grandmother now had a tree growing out of its roof. When she looked at the façade, she could still smell butter and fried meats fighting it out with perfumes and the aftertaste of hair spray. The bathroom had a bench in front of a mirror where she used to watch her grandma reapply her lipstick. Janine pressed her lips together now, smacking them in imitation. Sometimes her grandmother would even put a little on her. She loved the waxy feel of it on her mouth.

The east side she grew up on was in decay. There were plans for a Walmart. The shortcut to work would get crowded because of it. Squatters would be removed. Buildings would be torn down and replaced with Supercenters and new exits on Independence. But Janine liked it better as it existed. It was like those photos she'd seen of the ruins of Detroit Rock City, and somewhere above it all, the sign from Eastland, Charlotte's dead mall, that glorious puff-cheeked sun, still stood like Charlotte's version of a certain Dr. T. J. Eckleburg.

Janine remembered when she and Maddie used to walk the streets back there in between her dad's place and Family Dollar, how they'd pick up buckeyes for luck, search for coins to buy candy. She got Fireballs. Maddie got Lemonheads. She thought about the glow-in-the-dark stars that they'd stuck on her bedroom ceiling when they were ten, how her dad had bitched about having to scrape them off before he could sell the house. She missed that house and what she used to have with her friend Maddie. How they'd stare at that ceiling and talk in the dark, Maddie's voice drifting upward from her pallet on the floor. How Janine had told Maddie there—looking up at a plastic Androm-eda constellation, its deformed A-shape—that she was gay. She'd told her first, and Maddie said she knew, like it was no big deal. Janine loved her even more for that. She thought of watching *Clash of the Titans* on the twelve-inch TV in her old bedroom, the woman who played Andromeda, the slope of her neck, the way her white gown draped, how Maddie had told her she could be her twin. She giggled at the im-ages of the claymation Kraken and Perseus's awesome curls. She couldn't believe Maddie had had a thing for him. That movie was the reason they'd gotten into mythology and plastered those constellations on her ceiling. They talked of Andromeda's beauty and weakness. She was everything they didn't want to be.

Janine stuck her key in the door and took a deep breath. As she locked the door behind her, she surveyed the space. It was her favorite time of day, this time when she was alone in her store. She noticed a smudge on the mirror above the paperboard fireplace set up in an outdated living room spread. The red sofa that was too red, the gaping cover a constant reminder of bad decisions. The store. Celia. It was always Celia there in the folds of her mind. Today, she'd mark the sofa down fifty percent and hope someone would buy it. Paper towels squawked as she put some serious elbow into getting rid of the smudge. The place still smelled like carpet shampoo, artificial lemon, and the rosemary candles she kept stacked by the register. They sold well. Twenty dollars for a three-wick candle to give your home the illusion of the type of clean you weren't capable of. They reminded her of the plant outside her grandma's back porch, how her grandma once hung snippets in the kitchen window to dry, made sachets out of it with lavender. When she was a girl, Janine stuck her face in the window and examined the tiny buds, sometimes breaking off a piece and crushing it on her wrists so she could sniff it all day. She was careful not to wash her hands on those days. If her grandma were still alive, she'd get her advice on buying. Woman had the best taste in the family.

"Fabric is like people," Grandma Sue would say. "Some of it strong, some of it weak, but always true to its character."

Richard wouldn't be in until nine o'clock, so Janine allowed herself a little time to walk the store in the natural light. Her routine called for her to flip the lights on at the last minute, right before she unlocked the doors. She liked working alone in the quiet dim. Running her hands over the upholstery, the tabletops, she tested for dust and felt surfaces for defects. Picks in the fabric. Dings in the wood. Janine knew the pieces well. She would arrange and rearrange, most of the time without help, but today she was ready. Everything was in place. At ten o'clock, she'd open the doors for a cross breeze.

When she finished her inspection, Janine went back to the office to check her email and go over last year's figures. Ordinarily, she aimed to sell ten percent over the previous year, but now she practically had to sell half the store to survive another month, and Maddie was still living in her house, eating her food, smoking pot through her window, as if Janine didn't know. Now, Maddie had brought home two old Pomeranians. She had to get used to constant barking and the faint smell of urine and corn chips.

When Janine had confronted Maddie about her dog-walking and self-destruction, Maddie's shoulders had slumped. She'd become reclusive, had taken over Janine's space, spread her clutter like the dirty kid on *Charlie Brown*. Maddie became her undertow. Maybe she planned to live at Janine's house for good. Janine had stopped to look her over this morning on her way out—saw Maddie all twisted up in the sheets, dogs on her head, arms flung about, her mouth open, snoring worse than Janine's father. She had planned to wake her up to see if she'd come help at the store but had let her be, opting instead to see if she showed up on her own accord. Where was the girl she used to know? Had the divorce burned her up? Right before she left, Janine noticed Maddie had set the coffee pot up for her again as if that small gesture would make a difference. She left without pressing the button. Maybe Maddie would get the message. They had started living separate lives a long time ago.

After looking over the spreadsheets, Janine pulled a stack of red tags, a ball of string, and a Sharpie from her desk drawer, carrying them close to her chest with both arms until she got to the Montego Bay table. It sounded more Pottery Barn than it looked. Someone had painted the antique table, and everyone knows that ruins its value but Janine had purchased it from a woman at a yard sale for next to nothing. Normally, Janine didn't stop at yard sales outside of certain zip codes, but the outline of the woman's thigh in her blue running pants had been reason enough to pull over. The woman, Lily, had inherited the table from her mother, a bohemian who'd painted it in an act of rebellion—daughters of Southern belles were only waiting, after all, for the chance to squander pedestals for pit hair and bearded men or even bald-headed women with guitars. What Janine loved about the table was the way the diamond inlay pattern could still be seen under the paint. She liked to imagine its two lives, as if the table had performed a great act of will and cloaked itself in the pigment of its dreams, a little midlife crisis minus the affairs and heartbreak. She picked at paint flecks in spots where it had loosened, places where she didn't think people would notice, or where they thought it added character—around its joints and, particularly, the medallion at its knees. Unlike the red sofa, she didn't care if she ever sold it.

Back in the showroom, Janine placed the tags and string on the table and proceeded to write out the sale prices. For the bigger items, she found it behooved her to write the new price rather than the percentage off on the tags. People were bad at math. She got a calculator and scissors from the front counter and put on one of the mixed CDs Maddie had made for her back in the nineties. It was midway through Portishead's "Wandering Star." Janine bobbed her head and couldn't help but move her feet and spin on the way back to the table. It was an appropriate choice for Maddie. Janine could see Maddie working on the CD—her trademark clove cigarette and black boots, her tattoo of cardinals on a limb that grew up her spine and branched at her right shoulder. Maddie and that song, the same cachet, moving to the same blackness and its river while Janine had long ago settled into her spot. Unlike her parents. Unlike Maddie. Janine wasn't trying to leave.

Janine was best in the small interactions, the ten-minute episodes of selling someone a wing chair or the twenty minutes of showing someone how to space-plan their room with newspaper cutouts. She'd take the yardstick and the masking tape and make an aerial view of an eighty-inch sofa for the customer to take with them to the empty room that would make up their living space. When moments grew longer, that's where Janine had trouble engaging, staying present. She sat back down, taking a quick moment to rub a cramp out of her leg. She needed to be more patient with Maddie. To try harder. How does one know when to let a long friendship go?

She did the calculations for the tags. Forty percent off $1,299 equals $779 for the full-length red sofa. She decided to make one big sign for the candles, candleholders, and vases rather than do forty individual tags. She wrote 20% OFF in block lettering and colored it in so it would be thick and obnoxious.

Inevitably, someone would come in and ask if they were having a sale when the room would be peppered with more red than Christmas. "We sure are," she'd say. "And what can I help you find today?" It made her stomach lurch but open-ended questions were always better than the standard "Can I help you?" The answer to that question is always, "No, just looking." Unlike the people she had to see in her life on a regular basis, she tried to find a way to connect with customers; she'd comment on their shoes or their baby, making sure to use gender-neutral language just in case. Some moms go nuts if you screw up the gender of their precious little angels. Maddie had made that mistake more than once and had argued her case for adding a line of what she referred to as "gay" stuff. Maddie missed the point a lot.

Janine studied her customers. She paid attention to how

they moved, their language when talking about the Matisse print. She thought she could always get a sense of the customers' personal styles in relation to how they saw Matisse. Those in favor had a more modern sensibility, liked color, and seemed optimistic. Those opposed had a darker view of the world and tended to walk in neutrals and dark woods. Like herself. Celia loved Matisse. She said she'd read somewhere there was no fear and loathing in it, said humanity needed such faithful blue. Those who had no opinion generally needed someone to tell them how to run their lives. Folks with no opinion were Janine's favorite customers. She could convince them to redecorate entirely, and she used them as her own blank canvas, taking the opportunity to populate their homes with her point of view, her eye. Janine's new girlfriend, Linda, had no opinion.

Tables were forty percent off, too, and dining chairs fifty. Floor mirrors were only ten percent off because she didn't have many in stock and certainly didn't feel like helping load them into cars they wouldn't fit in. "Where Is My Mind" came on with its heavy snare. She banged the Sharpie, took a sniff, and sang at full volume, like she did when she was alone. About that time, someone knocked at the back. On her way to the door, she skipped in rhythm and drummed on a sofa cushion. She could see her father's cowboy hat hovering above the twelve-hour sale sign. She screwed with him a little by locking and unlocking the door to the beat. In the sliver of glass between the sign and the doorframe, she saw his sigh.

"Isn't that a little loud for this time of day?" he asked, removing his hat.

"My store. My rules," she said, locking the door behind him. He kicked his boots together, making sure to leave the debris on the mat. "Could you really hear it outside?"

"Hell, I could hear it coming up the walk."

"Guess I should turn it down a little. I don't want security up my ass."

"Got any coffee?" he asked, kissing her on the cheek.

"You can make a pot. Still got a bag of Christmas blend in the freezer."

"What, no Folgers?" he said with a smile, leaving his hat on a bedpost. "Store looks nice. You ready for today?"

"As ready as I'm gonna be. Need to get the tags hung. Rich will help with that when he gets in. You sure you're okay to help load furniture?"

"Is anyone else coming?" he asked, stretching his back.

"Well, I'd hoped Maddie and Linda were coming, but I didn't get confirmation from either."

"Great. How are things going with you two anyway?" he asked, walking off toward the break room.

"Maddie or Linda?"

"Well, I was talking about Linda, but what's up with Maddie? She okay?" he asked, opening the freezer.

"I'd rather talk about Linda. That's better than Maddie, but even that's not so great," she said, sitting.

The break room could barely hold two people. If they weren't careful, they'd bump elbows in the room cramped with a sink, mini-fridge, coffeepot, and microwave, all hand-me-downs from Janine's dad.

"I see the fridge is still working," he said, opening the door, taking a whiff. "It could use a cleaning though. It's got that old cheese smell."

"I cleaned it. That's just how it smells, Dad."

"So, Linda?"

He looked for the coffee filters to no avail and took his pocketknife to a paper towel folded three times over to use as a substitute. He dumped an unmeasured amount of coffee in, poured the water, pressed the button. He pulled one of the two chairs back as far as he could from the table, but his belly still touched the edge. Janine stared at the coffeemaker.

"Linda is Linda. In theory, she's good for me. Strong, quiet, a good cook. Stable. Linda's stable. And she dresses well. I wish I could get away with her clothes. They sort of look like Grandma's. I wonder sometimes if I'd like her as much if she wore ratty Levi's and T-shirts."

"Stable's not so bad. You sound like your mother," he said, cracking his knuckles.

"Bite your tongue. I'm nothing like her. It's just that, that—"

"You don't love her."

"Sounds awful when you say it out loud," she said, looking at the tiles.

"But you're going to stay with her," he said, trying to meet her eyes, without success.

"The truth is, Dad, I like the way she fixes my eggs. I can't re-create it. She scrambles them with a little dill and salt and pepper, but no matter how hard I try I can't get it right. I'd hate to give up those eggs because I don't think I feel whatever love is supposed to be."

He stood, pulled his jeans up a little. "Stop screwing with me."

"No, Dad, it's just, today is sale day. I can't deal with this right now. I have to finish getting the store ready."

"And Maddie?" he asked, with his back to her. The coffeepot beeped.

"I'm not discussing Maddie," she said, filling a paper cone with water and tossing it back.

"So, the Maddie situation is worse then?" He poured two cups of coffee. Fixed one with whole milk and lots of sugar and left one black. He handed Janine the black coffee, still trying to get her to look at him.

"Thanks," she said. "I'll let you know when someone needs help. I expect we'll be busy. You can hang here or in the stockroom. Please make sure you let me know if you leave for any reason or if you need help. I don't want you trying to lift a sofa alone. I'll send Rich back."

"I think you've got more heft than Rich, sweetie. Besides, that's what a hand truck is for," he said.

"Thanks, I guess?"

"Get to work," he said.

She hung tags at the front of the store, getting as far as the mercury table lamps and the jute rugs when Rich turned his key. He had a massive Red Bull in his hand. The first thing he said was, "Ready, Freddy?"

"Ugh. You really had to go there today?" Her eyes darted to the energy drink in his hand, then to the red slacks and penny loafers.

"You better believe it. These bad boys are my selling pants," he said, sticking his leg out and gesturing at them with his free hand. "I haven't sold less than $1,500 on any day I've worn them."

"You need to sell four times that today, buddy. We both do." She pointed to the stack of tags on the coffee table. "Grab a stack after you drop your stuff in the break room. We have a lot to do in an hour."

"Sure thing, boss ma'am."

"It's going to be like that, is it?"

He mouthed the words to George Michael's "Freedom" as he walked away. This was Janine's favorite mix. Depeche Mode was next. She'd have to put on something instrumental or maybe contemporary country before the store opened. Faith Hill and the like, for the customers. She hated that shit. She thought country music should die or sound like Johnny Cash, deep and harsh like the guitar strings were burning. Cash still wiped every pore clean, exposed every surface when she heard him sing. She couldn't listen to him often.

The last day Rich wore his lucky pants was the day her mother had stopped by. She had not waited on Janine to finish with her customers, but left a mocha for her at the counter. All these years later and there she was in the store trying to act like she hadn't left them, handing out chocolate-and-coffee penance. Janine guessed her mom had expected a phone call after that but she hadn't called. She'd driven by her aunt's house where her mother was living, but she couldn't bring herself to get out of the car.

She went to the office, picked up the Top 40 mix but stood there cleaning it for too long. Then, The Mamas and The Papas came on. Janine remembered Maddie in her knee-high boots, striped sweater, and miniskirt, leaning up against the Ford Festiva she used to drive in high school. She couldn't force herself to stop the CD. Janine hadn't decided whether to go to Linda's tonight. Linda was making a roast with Yorkshire puddings—her English family's weekend tradition. She could certainly handle such food after a long day. Gravy soaking into puddings could do a gal a world of good.

Janine had started to stay over at Linda's more and more. What started as a Saturday night date here and there turned into three-day stretches during the week. It was only a matter of time before Linda asked Janine to move in. But Janine liked her own house even though Maddie was still there— its long hallway, its sixties teardrop light fixtures drooping with heavy metals. Linda's house had fine things, hell. Janine had damn near furnished her whole house, but Linda's house wasn't home. Linda's house was sterile with white walls and beige carpet. Janine's house had hardwoods, a rug that belonged to her grandmother, mason jars and champagne flutes, old rosemary planted out back. She would have to start over at Linda's house. But Janine was starting to worry the problem was wider than where she lived. She felt she was losing something intangible at home, something she couldn't re-create at Linda's place or in Maddie's company. Both houses morphed into empty boxes, and she wondered if she'd ever get her security back.

A little boy in cable-knit blew on the front glass. Rich said he was on it and a moment later Janine heard the familiar squawk.

Business picked up in the afternoon. People had had their brunch, their own versions of Linda's eggs, and had wound through the shopping center, thinking about summer entertaining. Some people had seen the ad in the local alternative paper, *Creative Loafing*. Janine had splurged on a full-page ad for the occasion, having never done much advertising. Her dad had chipped in half. The store hummed. Janine found herself stuck at the counter ringing people up. She sold both the Tisdale chairs—deep leather with rolled arms. Those were both over two thousand dollars. Whiskey-stained leather fetched a premium.

"You know about how it scratches, right? The imperfections? I try to tell everyone before they purchase leather like this. Let me show you," Janine said.

The man and woman followed her to the front of the store, where Janine ran her fingernail over a small patch on the arm. The leather discolored like the underside of a leaf. "See. I want you to know what you're getting into. Leather seems sturdy enough, but it is prone to scratching and defects of hide, and it's not completely saturated with color. It's what I love most about it, though."

"We understand," the man said.

"We want character, too," the woman said.

The couple in matching sweater vests wanted character. Walking back to the register, Janine thought of Maddie sitting with her legs thrown over the arm, drinking wine from the bottle on one of those nights they'd spent at the store. Sometimes it was easier to be there—where they could rearrange rooms without commitment. On those nights, they talked of traveling the world. Maddie had spoken time and again about how she was going to leave that town, go somewhere more liberal, like she'd ever been involved in politics. She wanted to be with people who didn't think she was a freak, her mother's judgment, always present, crowding her perception of things. But in truth, they had to be careful not to offend. At the store, they were safe.

When she took fifteen minutes away, she found her dad back in the break room, munching a chocolate ice cream cone.

"I figure I earned it after that last one," he said. "That son of a bitch damn near fell on top of me. Rich doesn't seem to understand physics."

"You talking about the armoire? I can't believe someone bought it. One of the doors doesn't want to stay shut. It was sold *as is*, right? They knew that, didn't they?"

"They knew. Damn thing kept popping open when we were trying to get it in their truck. I finally got a bungee cord and wrapped it around the thing."

"Want some?" he asked, pointing the cone at her.

"Careful, Dad, the ice cream's going to fall. And no, thanks, I've got a Weight Watchers ravioli thing in the fridge."

"Gross," he said. "I never could eat those. I'm a Stouffer's man. Ever since your mother left."

"I remember. I think we lived off their lasagna with meat sauce."

"Sometimes we had mac 'n cheese and sliced apples."

"Sometimes that's all I have now. But I have to be careful. There's an awful lot of fat in those things."

"You don't have anything to worry about."

"You haven't seen my ass in a long time, Dad."

"You worry too much," he said, slapping his belly. "Look at me. We've all got our problems." His shirt was bulging in between buttons and sweat soaked through the plaid in spots.

"You sure you don't want to talk about Maddie?" he asked.

"I'm sure."

"Good thing," he said, looking toward the doorway. Maddie stood there in her one pair of dress pants, wearing beat-up shoes.

"Hey, Mad girl. Welcome to the ruckus," he said.

"Thanks," she said, her shoulders still a little slumped.

"I'll leave you two alone, but first, did you hear who bought the red sofa, over the phone no less?"

"No, who?" Janine and Maddie asked in unison.

"Your mother."

"Whose, mine or Janine's?" Maddie asked.

"Yours," he said, looking at Janine. He shoved the last bite of cone in his mouth and said, "Back to work."

"I wondered. My mother would never have bought a red sofa," Maddie said. "You need me to work the register while you help customers?"

The microwave beeped and Janine nodded without a word, watched Maddie walk away.

Back out at the register, they stood together for a moment before Janine returned to the showroom.

"You should think of investing in some new shoes. Are those the ones you used to wear to The Pterodactyl when we went dancing?"

"Yeah, they looked good with my fishnets. The only other shoes I had that weren't four-inch heels or tennis shoes were my Doc Martens, and I didn't think you'd want me wearing those."

"Remember the time I puked in the parking lot?" Janine asked.

"That was after Cel—the c-word, how could I forget?" Maddie said. Then, Maddie stopped and her eyes went up; she was listening. She recognized the song arrangement, that it wasn't what Janine normally played in the store. Janine knew she would. A gentle strum, a tap on a drum, a shake of a tambourine. Bob Dylan sang, somber and poetic as anything. Maybe their friendship would hold.

LAKE HARTWELL, SOUTH CAROLINA

It's past lunch hour and Grandmother is still wearing her housecoat. Tings and sprays bounce from the stovetop. A glimmer of steam gathers on her upper lip, not sweat, mind you—not sweat. The peonies on the fabric are wide and heavy pink, like they'd fall over if they were out in the side garden as they always are during late April. But we are in July and July is sweet and frayed, the grass only green down on the banks of the lake. Me and Juna played chicken on rafts all morning. Our suits still damp when we put them on, hers only halfway up as we ran out the door, letting it slam too hard, hearing Grandmother say, "Watch my nerves. For Lord's sake. My nerves." By the time we come in, we were striped, our torsos a wormy kind of white, our fingertips wrinkled, begging for fried squash and okra Grandmother had in heaps by this point, for smushed-up peaches meant for the ice cream churn, for teeth-cracking chunks of rock salt, the wayward bit of a watermelon seed, you know, that stringy bit you can't get down no matter how hard you try so you wind up spitting the seeds on Grandmother's floor even though you wasn't supposed to be eating them in the house cause y'all know better, cause she done told you twice to get your butts outside. And once you're outside, the menfolk stand in a circle around their cache, taking stock of M-80s and bottle rockets and whirling spiders and whistling dixies, which was basically the same, but hateful, so hateful you could feel it blow your cousin's pinky off even though some grown-up yelled "fire in the hole" and dumbass stood there in a sulphur fog like it was all happening to someone else and next year when you and Juna went in at lunch you were practically teenagers and ate rolled-up honey ham cigars and Chicken in a Biskit Crackers—those buttery rectangles with a chemical chicken flavor—instead of spitting seeds on the floor cause now y'all were good girls, making sure to let Grandmother lie down awhile and have herself a little peace in the back room with the big box fan and a single bed and her thin, yellow sheets.

SINKING AND SWADDLED

Ona left the day before her mother succumbed to a sinking disease. The two of them stood on the precipice of a black crevasse tying broom and mop handles together with kitchen twine so they might poke the bottom, but when Ona felt no resistance, no thunk in mud, no yielding to water, she knew grim days were ahead. Her mother read the signs, too, and shut herself in the bedroom, never to emerge.

Pleading, Ona said, "We'll find a safe place to sleep, Mama. You got to come with me. We got to make our own salvation. And it's out in the world, not behind this shoddy door."

But the sinking had already pulled her skeleton too hard, too fast—a steel frame at the base of quick-dry concrete. Ona did all she could. She whispered, "I always loved the way you brushed my hair slick, like I should be made of satin ribbon and tulle not square-built and sun-sour." She pulled purple chalk from her jeans pocket, drew a heart on the door, and gathered her things.

She swore she felt the earth drop—like a hitch in an ele-

vator—several miles from her mother's house. She thought
of all those bedlinens agitated, curled, heaped on top of her
mother, sunk along with everything else, beams, roof tiles,
the acrylic nails her mom wore, the senselessness of waste.
Her father had sunk, too. Years ago, in a prefab home out
on the lake. One day the lake rose a mite and the ground
dove a mite and from what her mother said, her father was
better off down there, probably still passed out on his leather couch. Ona had been swaddled and maneuvered into
the bow of a rowboat and, as legend tells, slept through the
whole affair. Perhaps it was this swaddling she longed for
more than anything with all this terrible sinking going on.

Ona walked for days, determined to find safety on higher ground. If she read her instruments correctly, she was adjacent to a national forest. The public would not stand for
the sinking of a national forest so when she found a slate
bungalow, she settled there. Though two walls were missing,
she concluded it was due to wind and rain and the birch tree
that had swindled its way up and through the middle of the
sweet, abandoned home. It wasn't sinking.

The kitchen still held a butcher-block table with a family
of plates. Ona piled them one on top of the other and pulled
them to her chest, sick with grief, sick with longing at the
sight of the dust-free circles left behind. After rinsing each
dish in the creek, she dried them with her shirtsleeve and
put them back in place. At dusk, fingertips numb, Ona tore

sheets of bark from the tree, building herself a papery cradle on the uneven floorboards where she could sleep for years.

TOMORROW OR TOMORROW

Navigating the Volkswagen in the rain took all Vicky Lee's concentration. Keeping both hands on the wheel, she closed her bad eye and squinted the other. Phil had offered to drive, but he'd been sipping codeine cough medicine. They were in desperate need of hot and sour soup. White pepper and rice vinegar–spiked broth to soothe the hack and spit, calm the beast making them hate each other for being sick at the same time. Somebody was supposed to take care of them. Somebody was supposed to be in the kitchen banging around. Somebody was supposed to be running their fingers through somebody's hair. Neither were naming names.

Vicky lit a cigarette in the car though she said she wouldn't. Promises had been made. If she quit smoking, he'd try to do better about helping around the house. Not leave noodles in the pot on the stove or garbage in the bedroom. Smoking was worse, he'd argue. Dirty dishes weren't going to kill anybody. He was always grading their mistakes.

"Jesus, man, bronchitis is no joke," Phil said, rolling down the window. The fever only increased her tendency toward self-destruction, but despite the unspoken urge to drive fast and hard toward the other lane whenever he spoke, she kept her foot ready over the brake, her gaze steady. There should be enough gas to pick up takeout and make it back to their apartment. Should be. They could use some of the laundry quarters if they had to.

They had to park on the other side of the lot from the restaurant. It was close to Christmas and folks were clamoring at Dollar General. Phil slammed the door, went to get the soup, dumplings, and sesame chicken she wouldn't eat. Families came and went. A father and son with a small bag for mom, the little guy grinning up at his dad, missing both his top front teeth and full of the kind of energy only little ones radiate this time of year. No matter how joyful adults try to make it with the buzz of packed schedules and a thousand ways to make things sparkle, it's always tinged with melancholy. Vicky had only realized in the past few years how much the holiday had cost her parents. All the extra hours which meant more time on the road for him. The extra strain on their marriage. The limitations of layaway. Her snooty-butt attitude about knockoff brands. She wished she could go back and behave better, show them kindness. Between shoppers leaving, she watched the green twinkle lights in the window at the Chinese place. Her legs sweated against the pleather. Every part of her was sticky from the humidity and she wondered what it meant when Christmas was turbulent like May, wet like June. The smoke from her second cigarette wasn't going anywhere; it sank down on her skin, looping itself through the steering wheel. She put her hand on her chest to see if she could feel tightness in her lungs from outside her rib cage.

Phil tripped on the mat outside as he walked through the door. His hair was freshly washed and the blond wisps behind his ears caught the green light, making him look horror or sci-fi or fantasy—an unreal genre of cool. He cursed, nearly dropping the bag. Vicky yelled as best she could, but it came out in squawks. "Drop that soup and it's your ass."

"Bring it, Punky."

He called her Punky after the show she loved as a kid, said she still had the same fashion sense, and looking down at her rain boots, *Family Guy* pajama shorts, and lumpy pig-tails, she couldn't argue.

"You know you'll never get well if you keep that up."

"I'm trying. They're as addictive as heroin, you know," she said, flicking the rest in a puddle.

"Fool who says that has never done heroin."

"Hardest thing I've ever had to quit. Maybe don't be a dick about it."

Vicky walked around to the passenger side and opened the door for him.

"I went in for the food, didn't I?"

"Whoop-dee-fucking-doo," she said, winking as he folded his long legs into the Celica.

Vicky also had a hard time shaking thoughts of her friend Cora this time of year. She'd been trying to push her out of her head all day. She knew she probably took some of it out on Phil, too. She was being unfair. It was right after Christmas 1991 when Cora had stretched herself out on the train tracks behind the mall. Now, everyone was celebrating the last Christmas before the millennium. Vicky and Phil had decided it was no big deal. Just another day. They were sick. They weren't teenagers. They didn't need anyone else. Besides, by the late nineties, half of their friends from high school had overdosed, done time, or pulled themselves apart in some other way. But there was still mystery surrounding Cora. She hadn't seemed the type. There was talk of an older guy giving her bad shit and dragging her out there to protect himself. Talk of her mama going to the apartment complex, banging on doors, crying to anyone who'd listen about her baby the track star. Mostly women answered. Mostly divorcées. Mostly recovered with two or three kids at their legs. But Cora's mom couldn't have known what the apartment complex was. She wasn't the type to see or give a damn about the unfamiliar. Vicky had been so jealous of Cora's mom, who always looked so neat compared to her own. She'd even go to the nail salon. Seemed like every time she saw her she had a different color. All Vicky knew was sometimes even young people had the urge to destroy shit, themselves included. She told herself the pack of smokes in her pocket was her last, and the booze at home she'd finish, but when it ran out, it ran out. She would get healthy. She'd start running. For Cora. For the rest of her lost tribe.

"Remember Cora?" she asked, one hand over the seat, looking back toward the lights.

"Like I could forget something so sick," he said, digging for a dumpling before Vicky slapped his hand.

"She laid herself down right in the curve so she knew the conductor wouldn't see her until it was too late."

"I remember. Total disaster."

"That sort of thing seems to be all along my periphery, babe. Consider yourself warned."

"I'll take it under advisement," he said, coughing into his shoulder.

"You sound like shit," she said.

"Maybe we'll die. Merry Christmas."

"Laissez les bons temps rouler."

"Wrong holiday."

"Whatever," she said, stealing the bag from Phil. "You know what I mean."

At the stoplight, a police car pulled up behind them. Vicky turned off the radio. Maybe Eminem wasn't the best impression for the cops, particularly when you considered her pink hair and his Nine Inch Nails shirt, forearm tattoos, and waifish frame. Sure enough, when the light turned green, the cruiser kept close. By the time they got to the pawn shop on Seventh Street, the blue lights circled and the siren came on.

"Pull in the parking lot at the pawn shop."

"Floodlights."

"Exactly. Probably cameras, too."

"I only have a learner's permit," Vicky said.

"Nothing we can do about it now."

"I'm stoned on cold medicine."

"Shh. Cry, if you can."

As the officer walked up, two more cars pulled in behind him. Like most white girls, Vicky couldn't believe it. She wondered if she was the bad juju for everyone in her life. A knock at the window, a demand, another demand, and they were outside the car, hands on the hood, legs spread, the Chinese food balanced between them. There was talk of white trash and pushing dope and questions about Vin from the restaurant. All they knew of Vin was his bracing manner, how he'd throw you out if you acted up, how pissed he got if you ordered dumplings, which took twenty minutes, how one time he gave them scallion pancakes because they seemed like good kids and he could tell they had only ordered soup because they couldn't afford the sesame chicken that day. It never occurred to them that he might be "slinging dope from New York." Not that they would have cared. Vicky guessed it was a tie between the fact that Vin was Asian and a New Yorker that pissed the police off most.

"We need a female officer."

"Sandra, come on. You pat her down."

Vicky could barely see Phil's face anymore. He'd hung his head. She wondered what her own expression looked like when the barrel-chested woman approached and ran her hand all the way up her shorts and the men behind her slapped her shoulder, saying, "Get it, girl." Vicky looked back at the twinkle lights in the restaurant window. If she didn't move, if she only saw the sparkle of green at a place she loved, she would be okay. When the female cop was finished, Vicky looked her in the eye, wondering why her mouth looked haunted when her hand wasn't.

"We only wanted soup," she said. In the span of five minutes, Vicky's fever had spiked and she'd sweated through her shirt. They said they should arrest her for sassing, let alone the permit and being visibly high. Phil sniffled, but Vicky couldn't tell if it was because he was upset, or because he needed to wipe his nose.

"Consider yourselves lucky, kids," the woman said. They warned Vicky and Phil to stay away from the restaurant and Vin. This meant giving up their favorite meal. Giving up the banter that comes with being regulars, letting go of the ease and comfort of rooster sauce and egg swirled into broth, the feel of seaweed between their teeth, losing the one place they wrapped their hands around ceramic cups of hot tea, their one place.

Phil drove them home. When they walked in, they still hadn't spoken. Vicky walked straight out to the back deck, white cartons of cold food in each hand. She spun hard in little girl circles until her stomach lurched, stopping only to launch each container off into the parking lot behind their building. It splattered all over a truck and ran down the windshield. Dumplings broke open. Phil didn't know what to do so he climbed up on the rail and stood there like he was waiting for some kind of answer. He coughed into his shoulder. It was Vicky who walked to him, leaning her head on the railing next to his feet.

"Let's walk the tracks," Vicky said. "I'll show you where Cora died."

"Punk, I think we need to talk. I don't think—"

"Better not. Let's save the catastrophe of us for another day."

"When?"

"Tomorrow or the next."

"Tomorrow or tomorrow."

"It doesn't even feel like Christmas."

"It hasn't felt like Christmas for years," he said, pulling one of her pigtails. "You should go to bed, Punk. Your fever's back."

Under two blankets, Vicky tried to remember what Cora looked like the first day of tryouts. Did she wear her mom's Tar Heel basketball shirt? The white Walmart shoes that looked like Keds? But all she could remember was Cora twenty yards ahead of her, limbs firing like mad, frizz curling at her temples, and the kind of woman she could have been.

LIKE AIR, OR BREAD,
OR HARD APPLE CANDY

At the corner of Palm and Flamingo, there is no sand or coconut-scented suntan lotion. There are no roof decks or boats waiting to be scraped and returned to sea. At the corner of Palm and Flamingo, there's not even the hope of an alligator float, duct tape–doctored, waiting to hold a fat-legged child. There's no sign showing the shortest route to the ocean is a whopping 222.7 miles, though Grenada had calculated it when she was a girl, asking Grandma why come their neighborhood had names like they was in Florida. Grandma's speech on the importance of names hooked there, forever in the soft spot behind her ear. There are, however, a good deal of lawn ornaments at the corner of Palm and Flamingo—worn-out roosters and a jockey who might have been black at one time tipped over next to a bird bath holding nothing but a pancake-sized circle of rainwater. It's old folks who live there, but Grenada doesn't see them much anymore. Used to be, when she was out with Petunia, her seventy-pound pit bull, she'd see them propping the front door open, both pushing walkers, moving the way octogenarians do, as though the whole world might give way beneath them. It must have taken them an hour to get to the car. She thought about helping, but the dog, you see. People were funny about bully breeds. Petunia tests Grenada's strength. Pulls so hard her shoulder burns. Lord in Heaven, she knows she probably should've gotten her one of those little dogs you can scoop up into a sack and throw on your shoulder like nothing, like air, or bread, or hard apple candy, a tallboy and a bottle of vodka, not that she was thinking about those things. Not anymore. The truth is she doesn't see too many of the people she remembers from the neighborhood. More moneyed people had started buying houses on Seaside and Sand Dune. She wonders what it means to walk past what used to be her great uncle's property and witness hulking machines smash in windows she used to gaze out of, particularly the one above the kitchen sink, where her aunt kept a lucky ceramic pig on the sill, where she'd pulled herself up and climbed over and cradled the little thing with its smiling pig face. What did it mean that she'd called it Petunia, too, and now the closest thing she'll ever have to a daughter peed on the lawn in front of the demolition? Grenada takes a big breath, the microscopic debris catching the rustle of autumn wind, leaves dry and brittle and caramel sweet, and wonders if she's taking in the last physical remnants of her long-dead relatives, a fragment of hair, a skin cell, some crumb of biscuit hidden under the fridge, never gathered, never cleaned, never consumed until now. But Petunia doesn't overanalyze. She follows the scent of some unknown creature, pulling Grenada away and up the hill until the only thing left for her to feel is the tingling of her own thighs.

TILLING

A light cloud cover, buds on the trees, and Good Friday around the corner. Dad said never to plant before Good Friday, to be clear of frost. Last year, I planted a bunch of heirloom tomatoes a couple weeks shy of Easter—Chadwick Cherry, Mr. Stripey, and Dr. Wyche's Yellow, varietals I'd ordered from the Seed Savers Exchange. And damned if they didn't just start to sprout good when we got a late freeze. I could've covered them with plastic sheeting or two-liter Coke bottles cut in half like I'd been taught, but I was full of myself.

Tilling took more upper body strength than I had. My thick-legged stance helped me control the contraption, but it inevitably got away from me, washing me in red dirt. I wiped my face with my shirttail and bent down to pull the tree root out of the tines. My youngest child, the only one still living at home, watched me from the window, so I play laughed like it was all such fun, like I wasn't mad as hell at the damn trees and bugs and dirt and everything. Tangled up in the mass, I found a statue no bigger than my hand.

He had a gash in his side but was otherwise intact. I pulled off one of my gloves and scratched the caked-on dirt from his face and robes. His eyes lacked pupils or lid delineation. Perhaps they were closed. His folded hands were themselves a prayer.

The only saint I could identify on sight was Francis, but he was easy. That downy lamb by his side. Bluebirds singing on his shoulder. This guy was no Francis. If I was Catholic and capable of turning saint, it's Francis I'd want to be. Pray for the voiceless. Cleanse myself of want or need. Let me sow love. Reframe the word *mass* to hold only positive connotations. Reduce its many definitions. *Mass* would no longer be something foreign housed in the dense flesh of my left breast. Or a group of angry protestors who were angry for good reason. Or a fearful priest performing the Eucharist. *Mass* would only be the number of atoms in this unknowable figure of a man and his level of resistance as I tossed him over the fence.

THE GOPHER IN RAE'S CHEST

Rae took care of all her husband's people. His parents and great-uncle all moved in when their house had finally caved in after twenty years of storms beating the hell out of their roof. She had stopped asking why they didn't do anything about the state of the place years ago, swallowed up the fact of her life of *have to* easier than she would a gel cap ibuprofen, which she had to buy in bulk when she realized the enormity of her household's collective aching.

After they were all in the ground, Hugh wanted to travel, but by golly she was tired and finally off the clock after thirty years teaching school and another ten feeding and tending to old folks. At least her parents had had the decency to die when she was a girl, her daddy sick from pesticides they sprayed in the fields, her mama from pneumonia, a complication from what they used to call emphysema. It seemed a stinking mustard plaster on the chest did not clear the lungs as well as penicillin. Rae told Hugh to let her be, that he could go off gallivanting any place he pleased, but she intended to rest for once in her life. She took to feeding birds. Making nectar for hummingbirds. Putting up suet. Black oil sunflower seeds in squirrel-proof feeders. She'd started putting check marks for every bird she saw in the Audubon book. She liked how they wiggled and shook in the bird bath, which she heated in winter months to keep from freezing over.

"Won't you come on and go with me?" Hugh said, picking up their plates. "I appreciate dinner. The beans were seasoned perfectly."

"Not interested."

"But you ain't never been anywhere," he said, spraying the heavy stockpot and lid he'd sprayed a million times before.

"And I'm good with that. What's got you so worked up? Better let that soak overnight," she said.

"Planning to," he said. "Can I interest you in any ice cream? Breyer's vanilla was on sale."

"You get chocolate syrup?"

"No, I didn't think to."

"No thanks, then."

"I'm sorry," he said, pulling the half gallon from the freezer. He scooped the ice cream like he was still a kid who wasn't allowed sweets.

"You ain't never seen much outside the state of North Carolina. Don't you want to know what else is out there?"

"Can't say as I do. What's got you so worked up? Wanderlust looks strange on you. Makes you sort of pink."

"Everyone's gone now," he said, before gulping down a big dollop of ice cream.

"Except me," Rae said, drying her hands on her apron. She'd gotten up to finish what he started while he continued eating.

"The house is too quiet. I can't hardly stand it."

She crossed to the living room and took a seat in Hugh's massage chair. "I like being able to hear the air click on. The barred owl at night is nice, too."

"Come on, Rae. Let's get an RV. You can listen to owls anywhere."

"Sure. Shove me in a tin can so I can still make your dinner even when I'm carsick and we're lost on some redneck highway to nowhere."

"We can't eat road food all the time. Cholesterol would skyrocket. That's why we'd take the kitchen with us."

"You should learn to cook, then," she said, crossing her arms.

"I love you. I'm only trying to get you out in the world."

"Oh, hush," Rae said, pushing herself almost flat in the recliner and letting the mechanism roll down her spine, highlighting all the little kinks she tried to put out of her mind during the day.

"What are you saying, exactly?"

"I'm saying you can't handle losing your people. They're gone and you feel like you're alone in the world. Like I ain't sitting here next to you. Like I haven't held your hand for most of my life. Like I'm what? You want to leave, that's on you. Go get you a recreational vehicle if you want. Spend the rest of your days in a bullet with wheels and sleep with one of those pullout sofa bars in your back. See if I care."

"You've gotten hostile in your old age."

"I'm tired, Hugh. That's all."

"Might as well be dead."

"Who's hostile now? I suppose you'll throw a tantrum, but babe, I got news for you—there ain't a thing on earth you can withhold from me that would make a difference."

"I'm going to the dealership."

"Go on, then. Pick up some eggs on your way home."

Still standing in the doorway, he turned around to face her, both hands in his back pockets, his shoulders raised, unsure. "I do love you. Same as I did the day you walked up Mama and Daddy's porch. I thank God for that barn cat of yours getting knocked up. For your tenderhearted Daddy trying to save those kittens."

"The man was a fool. Needed a lesson in farm mercy."

"Cats aren't livestock, Rae. They deserve better."

At that, Hugh's shoulders fell and he walked out the door to purchase his escape. Five hours later he came home with what Rae had to admit was a cute little number, had a green retractable awning and everything. For a moment when she stood next to her husband as he went down the list of all the knickknacks and doohickeys the thing had, she pictured the two of them on a hill above some lake cutting up hot dogs, frying them on a camp stove, pouring pintos in the pan and listening to them sizzle, replacing suburban air with wood smoke, and seeing the whole world turned blue in the fading light, but by the time he finished gushing, her flash of optimism had passed.

"It's pretty and all, but I'm not going anywhere in that thing. Pull the awning out and set up a couple folding chairs out here on the driveway and I might join you for ice cream or a drink in the evenings, but this bird is staying put."

The next morning, Hugh packed everything he wanted and that was that. Rae had the place to herself. She kept a similar cleaning and cooking routine for a few weeks but then figured what the hell and started letting things pile up. Wasn't nobody coming around. What did she care? She took to watching three soap operas in a row, stretched out on the massage chair, which she rarely left.

She was content for a time. She didn't shower if she didn't feel like it. She'd open the windows to freshen the place up but not every day. She refilled feeders when they were low and coordinated trips to the grocery store with trips to the specialty bird shop, where she talked with a nice young man in starched khakis about how to keep bluebird houses. But on one of her late nights watching *Designing Women* reruns, a pain burrowed into her chest like some kind of gopher, and before she knew it, she was on her hands and knees trying to force herself to take slow, deep breaths, to focus on the funny debutante thing Suzanne Sugarbaker did, but before long, she couldn't think about anything but calling an ambulance.

Chest pains get you seen quicker than most things. Her poor mama had died partly because they hadn't felt it was necessary to call the doctor in on the night she was admitted. They'd said her condition could wait until morning, but not Rae's. Hot lights on her face and a fast trip on the gurney made her nauseated or maybe it was the thought of being cut open after she had packed her mother-in-law's belly wound and changed her dressing. She hoped things would sort of fade to black, but they didn't.

In a couple of hours, they had her upright sucking on ice chips. Whatever they'd given her in her IV cooled her face and soothed the rodent in her chest. She had the nurse turn on the television. By then, it was the morning show circuit and all she could get was the one with that ninety-pound blonde with the squeaky voice, the one married to that good-looking fella on the soaps. They both used to be on soaps, but that gal thinks people forgot. The doctor turned the volume down when he came in to say her heart was fine; it was her brain on the fritz, said she might consider seeing a psychiatrist, get something to help, but in the meantime, here's five Ativan to help her sleep at night.

He put his hand on her shoulder. "Is there anyone I can call for you, ma'am?"

"Yellow Cab."

"We aren't quite there, yet," he said. "If you do okay for a few more hours, we'll talk about releasing you."

She watched ninety-pound Kelly hold herself so straight Rae thought she must be plopped down on a stick, like those expensive dolls her mother collected but never let her play with. She decided ninety-pound Kelly was better muted. Rae could make up her own story to go along with the guests. She pretended the guests were her own dead, come back to give a review of the afterlife, but all her father-in-law wanted to talk about was Hugh's recreational vehicle, catching mountain trout, hollering out at the gorge like a wolf, swimming a blue lake, charred meat. Maybe she was on the right drugs. Maybe she would see a shrink and ask for more.

The sun came in brighter than should be allowed in a hospital. Nurses came and went, but she hadn't seen a doctor since the one who told her she was crazy. She heard someone with squeaky shoes coming down the hall, but didn't expect it to be Hugh who turned the corner. He was tan, had buzzed what was left of his hair, and had trimmed down considerably.

"Well if it ain't the wild man of Borneo come to haunt my dreams?"

"Hey there, Rae. How are things? Doc says you had a scare."

"Everything's fine. I'm not dying. Just crazy."

"Don't talk that way," Hugh said, pulling up a chair. He slid the remote control out of her hand, set it on the rolling table, and placed both hands on hers. "I've missed you."

"Bull," Rae said, keeping her eyes on the screen.

He turned her chin his direction. "Rae, please. I'm having fun out there, yes, but it ain't the same on my own."

"I'm sure you could find some old lady, or hell, even a young one to keep you company."

"Stop."

"You stop."

"Anyway, I'm here to get you home and settled."

Hugh had brought her a change of clothes since the doctor told him they'd had to cut off her sweatshirt. He helped her get her arms in the long sleeves and pulled it gently over her head, smoothing her hair once it was on.

"I bet I look a mess. What'd you bring this shirt for?"

"Because you always looked good in peach."

"My slippers?"

"Right here," he said, pulling them out of his back pocket.

Once Hugh got the shearling booties on her feet, Rae felt cozy for the first time since he'd left. At first, she thought it was having someone around, but by the time he brought her hot cocoa that night, rubbed rosemary oil into her stiff shoulders, and made her rubbery scrambled eggs in the morning, she knew it wouldn't have eased her mind if it had been anyone else.

While he washed and folded his clothes, she walked out to the RV. She pulled herself up the steps and inside, where she opened all the cabinets, peeked in the bathroom, which only had a little soap scum on the shower door, and eventually lay down on the bed in the back. She wondered what it was like to arrive at a camp at night and open the window in the morning to an unfamiliar landscape. She wondered what ninety-pound Kelly and Suzanne Sugarbaker would say. She couldn't picture either of them under mosquito netting, going rogue without makeup, or having no agenda.

"What's going on in here?" Hugh asked.

"Hell," she said, jerking up. "You scared the bejesus out of me."

"This is my place, ain't it?"

"Wanted to see what it was like. It suits you, actually."

"It could've suited you, if you'd given it a chance."

Rae fiddled with her dress, feeling the gopher poke his head up out of her heart. "I think I have to tell you something."

"Yeah?"

"This gopher in my chest tells me I miss you."

"Does that mean you want to come along?"

"The gopher says yes."

"What about resting?"

"I don't think I can rest without you, but you know, they say I need medication so what do I know?"

"I should think so if you've got a gopher in there," he said, placing three fingers where he could feel her rapid heart.

"Can we pull the awning out tonight? It's supposed to be cool. We could light a fire."

"And I could play my harmonica."

"Or we could stay right here," she said, pulling back the quilt and sliding underneath. Snuggling into a bed that smelled like him again made her think maybe she wouldn't have to wipe his mouth or watch his toes purple near the end. Maybe she would die first after all.

AIN'T NOTHING BUT FIRE

Hardy's elbow cracked as he lifted the bucket out of his truck bed. With his father's fishing pole in his other hand and his keys between his teeth, he had too much to carry, but this is how he went about his mornings these days—loading up for the moment he could drop that lure in the opaque Atlantic. His feet crunched on sandy asphalt. Juniper, the hippie girl from Charleston, propped open the window of her Airstream trailer where she sold snow cones. Hardy loved how she kept her dirty blonde hair in braids and never wore a bra. During the height of the season, she often had a line twenty people deep. Hardy couldn't resist the mango himself. Yesterday, Juniper had remarked how Hardy's hair had gotten blonder than hers. His skin had toughened and darkened as well. But he was most proud of his feet, newly callused from going barefoot so much.

"Finally starting to look like a local there, Hardy," Juniper shouted as she wrote the day's flavors on her whiteboard.

"Before long, I'll braid it," he said, stroking his beard.

He waved hello to Frank, the young boy who worked the

tackle shop summer weekends. He had on his Gamecocks T-shirt. Much to his parents' chagrin, he planned on studying engineering there after he graduated next year. How a Clemson family produced a Cocks boy was beyond Hardy. Those people took their allegiances seriously. Hardy didn't care about any of it. He never went to college or got into college ball.

The pier was quiet. It was early fall and the kids had all gone back to school. Tourists receded and swelled back into their regular lives in office buildings and neighborhoods hours north of the low country, where the land rolled and rose steadily, where great cities smashed themselves together in the thick of winter. Under footfalls of gray snow, cars froze to the streets. Hardy had lived four hours northwest in Charlotte his whole life. These few months since he'd left it all behind and wound himself around his totem (the fish) had been the most content of his life.

He couldn't wait to spend his first fall and winter by the sea. He'd been to the beach once in January and had loved the desolation of the abandoned vacation houses and the feel of his boots sinking in sand, the sharp wind on his face, the lulling motion of the waves, the driftwood, shells left uncollected, and dunes developing heft. That was shortly after Loretta had left. He tucked Janine in at his parents' house one night after knocking back a few and got in his truck and drove. His parents understood. He was broken-hearted and terrified of raising a child on his own. He had rolled up to the pier at sunrise, saw the real fishermen packing up after night fishing, and sat there smoking with the windows down for hours. He took his time getting out of the truck. But he'd eventually opened the door and stumbled down to the beach, pulling his camo jacket tight around his chest and wishing for a thick pair of gloves. He sat on the dry sand and watched the tide come in until he was too cold and numb to stay there. Afterwards, he'd gone to a fish shack to warm up, where he had a bowl of she-crab soup with the right amount of heat to it to make both his eyes and nose run. It was the first time he felt truly separate from Loretta. It had finally sunk in sometime before the feeling came back in his hands. Sometime before he slurped his soup, the divorce became real. His buddy had a trailer over at the campgrounds where he stayed. That night, he got drunk and drove his golf cart around the property, cutting corners too fast and smashing bottles as he finished them. All he was missing was a big hound dog next to him, sliding around on the seat. He left the next morning for home and Janine, but that day had always stuck with him. He guessed that's why he'd picked Myrtle Beach.

Waves ate his line. A few tugs, but nothing stuck. He wound it up, checked his lure, stuck fresh minnows on the hook, and cast back into the sea, one time nearly taking a woman in a pink jogging suit's neck along.

"Whoa. Watch it, mister," she said, giving him a look that could've melted his face like the Nazis in *Raiders of the Lost Ark*.

Hardy hated it when women came up there in the morning. They were almost never there to fish, save for Doris, who came about once a week in knee-high rubber boots and a John Deere hat, with a slab of chaw tucked in her lip and a Gatorade bottle to spit into. She lived only for herself. She'd been arrested once for assaulting her cheating ex with a bucket to the head. Her ex had later dropped the charges provided she gave her a divorce. She'd told her nothing would make her happier. At least that's how she told it. Hardy didn't know what to believe, but he liked a woman who chewed tobacco. That was a statement right there. Womanhood takes all kinds. Doris and Hardy shared a bench from time to time, where they'd sit in silence, watching the poles and the lines almost intertwine. Like Hardy, she could sit and be. They didn't need to talk, but their bodies warmed when resting next to each other. Maybe if Loretta could've sat still for five minutes like that she wouldn't have turned everything to shit.

The clouds rolled in, giving his scalp a break from the sun's scorch. The surfers tired of waiting for waves and packed it in. He thought of his mother when they used to come for family trips when he was a kid, how she would bring a pillow and something to cross-stitch down to the shore. It had embarrassed him something awful, his mother lounging back on a satin pillow, smoking and sewing. She hated to get sandy or wet and didn't like to freckle. She put her hair up in a scarf to keep the sun from bleaching it or burning her scalp, and she seemed a nervous wreck whenever Hardy would get near the water.

"Look out for jellyfish and sand sharks," she'd say when digging through her box of thread. "I don't want to spend our vacation at the hospital. The last thing I need is a one-legged boy."

His dad would set his chair within toe's reach of the water and dig his cooler into the ground a little and drink until he emptied it and fell asleep. Inevitably, his fair skin burned and his mama spent the evenings coating him in sticky aloe.

Hardy had stopped drinking. These days he wanted to keep a clear head. The days were worth it, and nights he'd learned to relax out on the dock behind his house. The sunsets were getting more brilliant as the summer waned. Shades akin to salmon belly set his spine upright. No more slouching. He worked jobs when they came up but it wasn't a nine-to-five type deal. The season for work was in the fall and winter mostly, from what he understood from his boss. They didn't like to do too much construction during the peak season. Work would pick up soon, but for now he relished the drip of his days, one running into the other. He hadn't spoken to Janine as often as he'd wanted. But the girl had to figure out life on her own. He had given her the house so she didn't have a mortgage to pay once she sold her place, and he figured that was as much as he had left to give. He hoped she'd come to visit again, but doubted she'd come back after she realized his new place was a dump.

When the line pulled, he tugged and reeled. Whatever was on the end of it didn't weigh much. He felt it flitting as he continued to wind the line. He grabbed the creature with his free hand as he held the pole under his arm. A baby shark, about twelve inches long. His rounded snout and small eyes made him think it was a bull shark. Where the hook had caught in his upper jaw, the flesh had already turned purple. He wriggled in Hardy's hand, but he didn't let him go right away. The little thing could grow to be seven feet one day. Bull sharks were aggressive and swam in shallow water. He stuck his pinky in its mouth and felt the serrated teeth. It could probably take a big hunk of finger if Hardy didn't have control of him. He looked at its eyes. Every bit of a baby. Scared. Fighting. He cut off the end of the hook that had poked through and pulled it back out. Hardy sniffed his thick salt-skin and dropped him back into the water. Leaning over the railing, his stomach churned as he thought how his mouth would ache, how vulnerable he would be.

Hardy didn't catch anything else. Doris hadn't showed and even the surfers lacked enthusiasm. Salt and sand and weather had scored the wood on the pier, marked it, chewed it, and left it splitting and warped. He wondered how the structure survived hurricanes. All it would take was one good storm. He packed his things and walked from the end of the pier back to his truck. He took his smokes off the dash and lit one and sat for a moment on the back of the truck, remembering that cold day when his heart was so raw and how he'd never completely gotten over Loretta. They'd spent a fully clothed night together before he'd left. It had been the most real night of their relationship and it was a good twenty years after their divorce. She'd kissed him, and he'd felt it. Her lips were there in that moment; they pushed him against the truck, this truck. He'd wanted to take her back inside, to strip pretense off her, to feel how her body had changed. He could see it in her skin. It had started to get that crepe look he remembered from his mother's legs. But he hadn't. He'd let her go. He'd let it all go. She was coming down for a visit and he waited, wondering what would come of it, if they'd have the same connection, if she was still sober, how she was doing, if she'd made any progress with Janine, if she still slept on a mattress on the floor, what she'd think of the king-sized bed he'd bought for himself and the house itself. It was so different from his father's.

When he got home, he pulled up in what one would ordinarily call a yard but what was truthfully more of a sand patch with a thin gravel driveway. It was a small, two-bedroom house. There was no porch. There were no flowers, only a small oak out front with one clump of Spanish moss hanging down from the lowest limb. He kept meaning to pull it off. It made the space seem too romantic and he sure wasn't looking for anything resembling nostalgia or some bullshit charm tourists spoke of. He wanted the flat, sandy earth and the stink of wetlands when it got over eighty degrees. No other place on earth brought the smell of rot and rebirth so close. He put his fishing gear in the shed and locked the padlock. There'd been break-ins. People loved to steal mowers and lawn equipment, but Hardy didn't even need to bother with a mower. Sand out front and marsh out back didn't require mowing, but still, he didn't want his dad's fishing gear or his tools stolen.

He passed by his hammock, though he wanted to stop and nap, and went inside to clean for her. She didn't care much about a clean house but he wanted her to feel comfortable. He wanted her to see how it reflected who he was separate from everyone else—how he'd finally made his own way. There was no dishwasher in his bungalow, but he had a wooden drainer up on the counter where he'd set his coffeepot and mug to dry before he'd left that morning. He wiped the spots off the carafe and put it back on the burner. He filled his mug with Mountain Dew. No one was there to stop him and he didn't care anymore how bad soda was for him. The thick tang of citric acid and high fructose corn syrup was all right by him. He knew Loretta was bringing bad news, and that caught in his mind as he opened windows and dusted end tables.

He had no television anymore. He read in the evenings when he tired of walking and sitting on the dock. To save on electricity, he lit candles at night, so he'd lined his mantle with jars of them. The flicker looked peaceful and even though he'd read about the number of lumens one needed to read, he got by. He liked thinking he spent his evenings like someone in the nineteenth century, the sound of pages turning and the occasional snap of a candle the only breaks in silence. He'd fall asleep sometimes before he blew out the candles and he'd wake up sore on the couch and in a panic, worried about fire, and then he'd remember that's why he bought the candles in glass and so what if something did catch on fire; there was nothing in there he gave a proper damn about anyway.

As Hardy made the bed, he second-guessed his off-brand fabric softener. Maybe the manufactured mutant flower smell would dissipate before Loretta arrived. He hoped she wouldn't mind sleeping with him since he didn't have anything but a few boxes of books in the second bedroom. Most of his stuff went to Goodwill before the move. The only new thing he'd bought himself was the bed. Janine had recommended what she called Shaker style—clean lines, nothing fancy, stained walnut. She had said he needed a taller headboard since he sat in bed reading so much; he needed something to lean his pillows against so he wouldn't lose them behind the bed. She was right. When he managed to move to the bedroom before he fell asleep on the couch, it was the perfect reading spot and he could stretch out spread-eagle if he wanted to.

Loretta showed up not too long after he'd started reading Steinbeck's *Cannery Row*. He had remembered it from his boyhood but thought he might enjoy it more as a grown man. He was interested in the Palace Flophouse, the house where the wayward men seemed to gather to get away from wives and responsibility. He liked that they decorated it with found objects—rugs and tables and chairs and mattresses. He understood Mack, and when he read the book, he felt the urge to buy that motorcycle he never bought and sleep in the dirt by campfires.

Maybe he didn't want to be a drifter. Maybe he only liked their stories. He could make his house more bohemian like Mack and the boys, but he had to admit he was happy with the sparseness of the walls and the lack of curtains and the fact that it had no dentil molding or gaping cracks in the plaster. When Loretta came in, she commented on it right away.

"Your place looks like mine."

When he looked at her bull-shark eyes, he knew she was sick. "Do we give up on all that decoration in our old age or what?" Hardy asked.

"I don't know. I guess we know more about what works and what doesn't. What makes a life and what makes the appearance of a life. I don't know about you, but the thought of matching backsplashes and freshly stained decks, pedestal sinks, granite countertops, and lace curtains makes me want to slit my wrists."

"You always did have a way with drama, Loretta. I don't know if I'd go so far as to say that. It makes me jittery, I guess," he said, putting his hand on her shoulder.

"That why this place is so empty?"

"It's not empty. I got candles and books and coffee paraphernalia."

"Too bad you don't have other paraphernalia."

"You wouldn't break your sobriety, would you?"

"I don't know. Shit's changed since—"

"I don't want to know darlin'. Not yet. Let's be together a while. Spend an evening, you know."

"I don't really want to talk. It's just—it ain't nothing but fire, is it?"

"What ain't?"

"This life, right?"

"Beats me."

"Well, to hell with it. How about a tour?"

"There ain't much to see as you can tell from the grand entrance." He gestured to the living room. "Couch."

"Same old couch," she said, picking up one of the flat throw pillows and hugging it to her chest.

Hardy walked down the short hall, scratching the wall as he went. Loretta followed. "You hear from Janine? I still haven't."

"I talked to her about two weeks ago. She was busy working, trying to drum up business for the store, but I don't think it's going to last much longer. That ex-girlfriend of hers, Linda, did you ever meet her? Woman threw a brick through the front door." He opened the door to the second room. "Spare room."

Loretta nodded. "No kidding? Did Janine press charges?"

"No, she felt bad breaking the nut job's heart. It's too bad. I liked her a lot better than the one she was batshit over a few years back. Linda loved our girl, but Janine kept her at arm's length. I guess she's still waiting on the one that ain't coming back. Girl can't appreciate what's right in front of her." He turned around to the master bedroom. "Master," he said. "And the only bath is in there. There's a tub if you want a bath later."

"You can't force love, though, Hardy. You know that," said Loretta.

"Is that what happened to us?"

When she didn't answer right away, Hardy had to get out of the hall and back to the living room.

"You know I loved you, Hardy. I was messed up back then. Self-medicating and self-destructing."

"Beached whales and the like," he said. "Wanna see out back? It's my favorite spot."

As the sun went down, a blue heron stood out in the marsh, one-legged, meditating on God knows what. Hardy reckoned it was full on fish and feeling content with the world, its foot squishing down in the muck, crabs scurrying about and insects buzzing on the wind. He understood. Loretta reached for Hardy. It wasn't until he felt her hand that he noticed how thin she was.

"Let's get you some dinner," he said. "Should I cook for you or do you want to go out?"

"Let's stay in. Do you have anything to fix?"

"I got some catfish and corn in the freezer and a can of biscuits in the fridge."

"That sounds fine to me," she said, "Can we grill the corn out here?"

"Yeah, charcoal's in the shed. Do you want to fry the fish inside or should we bring a pan out here?"

"I'll do it inside. You got flour and cornmeal?"

"I think so."

Loretta stayed inside and coated the fish in the flour, cornmeal, salt, and pepper. Hardy didn't have an iron skillet, just a small nonstick frying pan, so she fried the fillets in two batches. It didn't get as crispy as they liked, but it would do. With the last of it on paper towels and the biscuits browned, she took two plates, plasticware, and the food down to the dock on a big sheet pan. Hardy plopped the charred corn down next to the fish. They ate off each other's identical plates until both were empty. They laughed about how neither of them was good at cooking back when they were a couple.

"Poor Janine!"

"How'd she wind up with parents like us?" Hardy asked.

"God knows," she said, putting the trash in a pile. "Or maybe God has nothing to do with it. We were clueless. Like everyone, I suppose. Got a cigarette?"

He pulled the pack from his back pocket. "Here. But you're only allowed one."

"Like hell," she said. "How do you stand the smell out here?"

"I've gotten used to it. I like it."

"You like the stink? That burning in the back of your throat?"

"It reminds me to stay in the moment. And yes, I do. It feels more like home than Charlotte ever did."

"I guess I know what you mean," she said. "For me, it's like how the forest smells in the mountains. Late November, after rain and fog have thrown a blanket over everything and turned it to compost."

"Yeah, something like that. But the sea makes it different.

It's not myth. It's not folklore. It's death out there in your face. Like this book I read that talks about how the shells and the beach itself ain't nothing but a cemetery."

"You and your books."

"My books make me happy. What makes you happy these days?"

"I'm not sure happy is in my vocabulary, but I guess I'm content with where I am now, in Charlotte, trying my ass off to get my life together, to reach Janine, to set up living on my own, like you. You're my best friend, Hardy. You always were. That's why I'm here."

"I know, babe. I know."

They rode down to the ocean. It was the time of year when you could drive on the beach after sunset and build bonfires. They parked with the back of the truck toward the water and sat in the bed. A group of college kids were drinking and dancing around a fire about a hundred yards up the beach. Hardy wished he'd done something like that when he was that age but when they were that age, they already had an infant to care for. The temperature dropped faster than they expected. Loretta's hair whipped Hardy's face.

"Want me to put on some music?"

"Nah, I like listening to the waves and the kids."

"I wish we had a joint. I had a regular hook-up back in Charlotte, but I haven't been brave enough to ask anyone

I've met down here. I don't want to give off the wrong impression."

"A joint would do me right."

"What is it, Loretta? Tell me."

"Cancer," she said, looking off toward the fire.

"Is it bad?"

"Bad as it gets."

"I had a feeling," he said. "I figured when you said you had something to tell me and it had to be in person."

"No one else knows yet. Not even my sister."

"When are you going to tell everyone?" he asked, rubbing her shoulder. She didn't answer.

"You cold?"

"A little," she said. He wrapped his jacket around her and she slid her arms inside.

He opened the door for her and put her in the truck after an hour or so of sitting in silence. He understood where she was coming from. He'd been through this with his dad. He'd seen all kinds of reactions to bad news about one's health. But Loretta wasn't lashing out like she would have when she was younger. She sat close to the door. Like a blind dog with her head almost out the window, mouth open and wind stinging her snout.

When they got back to his house, he lit candles and got out his ratty afghan. They curled up on the couch, watching shadows bounce on the white walls, saying nothing. He kissed her and they moved into the bedroom. When she climbed on top of him, they moved to a familiar rhythm, only this time there wasn't so much fury in it.

Afterwards, he lay there, smelling her sweet corn breath. Both of them knew he wasn't moving back to take care of her.

He'd made his life there in Myrtle Beach. He was bound to it, caught up. He had severed the shared limb between him and Loretta that day years ago when he sat on the winter beach. She knew it. She needed his strength to propel her forward. To carry these moments with her into her treatments. Into the hospital for surgery. Into the infusion room. Into machines and waiting rooms. When she counted backward from one hundred, she'd smell marshland and see biscuits and fish on paper plates, a plastic fork held by a man she loved.

PRESERVATION

Lula took a double, sent word to Katrina's school for her to ride the bus, the child's face a perfect melt of disappointment for the year since she'd accepted the job at the diner. But it was close to home and open twenty-four flexible hours. Though Lula smelled like butter-flavored oil, she fixated on her marigold uniform and frilled side cap, pinning it just so before each shift. If Lula weren't so tired from running armfuls of plates like a Corelle-ware ballerina or so guilty from Katrina's incessant floor-gazing, she might have felt cute. The child had a key and knew the rules about anybody who come knocking or calling or asking for anything. She'd already been grounded for running off with Jenny, the other kid in the complex whose mama was on her own. But what good was punishment without an enforcer? Lula couldn't sling pancakes and make sure the girl stayed in her room, working math problems she didn't understand.

A few hours after dark, Katrina showed up, tapping on the window, waving her mom outside, but Lula told her to get her ass home. "I'm slammed, doll," she said, as she rolled an ankle and lost a bowl of banana pudding. "Please," she said. "Mommy can't right now."

"Mommy never can," the girl said, pulling her hood up and over her eyes.

Every time she worked late, Lula held her breath when she turned the key in the lock. The lock that stuck on humid days. The door that had almost been padlocked more than once. The dank bottom floor apartment of a split-level where the whole damned world was less shiny. Windows only on one side—they were bricked into mud on the other. Jenny at least lived on the top floor, dappled light flitting all around her mattress on the floor. Tonight, Katrina had left the light on at the kitchen bar, their only eating space. Lula pulled up the stool, which had fit at the last place only to be too short here. The pendant warmed a mud pie housed in tinfoil, decorated with a single pinky-sized skull in the center. Katrina hadn't made a mud pie since before her dad left. She was too old for such nonsense.

"Baby? Can you come here a minute?"

"I'm supposed to be sleeping," Katrina yelled.

"Get in here, please. Explain yourself."

She twirled her hair at the temple until her scalp pulled. "What, pray tell, would you like me to explain?"

"That," Lula said, pointing to the tiny, white-horned thing.

"It's the skull of a pygmy horned lizard."

"My Lord, child. Why?"

"Why what? Why is it here? Why does it exist? Why is its crown so perfect? I found it taped inside a book in the library. I couldn't leave him there alone. I thought about the doe we watched get shredded by vultures next to your work so I brought him home. Lizards like him burrow, you know. I gave him back his mud."

FLY THE CAR TO MARS

Before we left the house we shared with Grady—the last of a long string of Mama's weirdo boyfriends—she started taking pictures. So many I almost never saw her brown eyes anymore. She'd found an old Canon in Grady's basement, the manual type manufactured long before anyone could have wrapped their heads around pixels or smartphones. Mama followed me to the bus stop, shooting the sky and leaves, dandelions and roadkill, and always always if it was warm enough to wear shorts, the crook of my knee, the bruises on my shins from fighting other girls and half the boys, the way my jean shorts frayed, the marker-drawn hearts on my back pocket, and always always in black and white. She talked about contrast and exposure and film speed and movement and wasn't it glorious what we could do in the modern age, babycakes? Black and white squashes the warmth out of things. No more heat in the sunrays. No more pink skin. No more chlorophyll or hell, anything on the whole ROYGBIV wheel.

I'd sit on the curb picking at scabs, wishing we could

live somewhere just the two of us, away from these men she took up with, but she'd tell anyone who'd listen (the grocery store people, the drive-thru bank people, the power company people, my teachers, and that gray suit lady who came from social services when one of my so-called friends told how Mama left me alone sometimes), we were doing fine, thanks for the inquisition, and in the next breath she would let loose on whoever had the dumb idea to ask.

"Lord help you and your fancy ass. I hope you don't ever have to stick one stinking pinky toe in these shoes. You don't know what life is, kid," she said to the gray suit woman. "Talk to me when you've been left and beat and cheated on and had to decide between heat and power, food and gasoline, your meds or hers, and when she turns the right way in the right light, damn if the kid ain't the spitting image of her backwards father."

Mama told the lady it's a real shit show trying to raise a child, especially a daughter, on your own, but I always tried to make myself as small and quiet as possible. I cooked myself eggs and toast. I ran the vacuum. I tried not to be expensive and learned not to ask for things if there was a way I could manage without bothering her.

But it's hard to make yourself small when someone's always got a lens pointed at you.

"Come on, baby. Look at Mama."

"I'll be glad when you get tired of taking pictures." The

bus was late and I'd be rushed on my pre-algebra test. Equations made me dizzy so I had studied and done practice tests and even tried sleeping with the textbook tucked under my pillow. Somebody told me about osmosis. I didn't take much stock in it, but figured with the noise of Mama and Grady going at it last night and the way my head seemed to float away from my neck when I thought too hard about letters representing numbers, or his greasy hands on her, it was worth a shot.

"Please," she said, sitting back on her knees in the middle of the road like it wasn't time for folks to go to work and school. She lifted the camera up to her face again, and the way she cradled it in her left palm with her pointer finger over the button bugged me. She cared for it, for a dang hunk of metal and glass.

"Fine. But only if you tell me what happened last night," I said, trying again to stare the black hollow of her lens down until I could send it flying into the storm sewer, but it seemed I was not telekinetic no matter how much I doodled Jean Grey on my paper bag book covers.

Behind the lens, her body stiffened, and she swung the camera over her shoulder in a movement so quick I barely had time to register what had happened.

"That's not your business."

"I live there, too. It's like y'all don't notice."

"You've got a room of your own, don't you? Food to eat?

You're judging from a place of comfort, hon. One day you'll see, but you'd better toughen up. Soon."

"I take care of myself," I said, picking my backpack up off the curb. The air brakes on the bus squawked as it turned the corner.

"Right. Dust a few tables, make your own bed, that's the same as working till you can't see straight to pay basic bills. That's the same as raising a child alone."

I wanted to say, what's the difference when I'm always on my own, when you don't talk to me, when you don't explain what it means to be a girl or how to do anything but try to go about my day unnoticed, and when that doesn't work because of my ill-fitting clothes or my buckteeth, that I start fighting. Break an older boy's glasses. Scratch a girl's face with my keys because she's prissy and has expensive shoes. Get called to the principal's office over and over. Talk to more grown-ups in suits. Tell them everything is fine, that I've never seen Mama take a punch, that she's always home by six o'clock, cooking chicken. Tell them no, my father isn't in my life, but we're totally dandy over at Grady's house. Grady provides. And when they ask me if he's good to me? I say yes, and tell them about the bedroom I have all to myself, but don't say that I feel like the other kids have it better and sweeter with moms who wear aprons, who look like the Disney Cinderella at the start of the story, all blue-eyed and humble, how everyone else must have birds and butterflies perched on their chests and honey on their breath. I don't tell them how I cover my head with an Army green Kmart comforter, trying to drown out Mama and Grady, unable to tell the difference between love and rage.

But what I really said was, "I'm sorry, Mom. I know it's hard," as the stop sign on the bus fanned out. Before I finished talking, she'd taken another picture and I feared what she might see on my face in that moment.

She squeezed my shoulder and turned toward Grady's house, but before she made it far, she said, "Hey, let's go get these developed when you get home. Caroleen says we can go with her to the darkroom at her community college."

"Maybe," I said. "Depends on how the math test goes."

"Break a leg," she called, without knowing the phrase is meant for putting on plays, not getting a headache over when to move what number where and solve for x.

When I got home, the house was quiet enough to feel the shag carpet sucking all the world's energy into itself. We read *The Outsiders* last month and I still thought about bad families and running away. But I wouldn't go to an abandoned church—that wouldn't be much of an improvement. I fantasized about living in the mall, about moving into Sears. Setting myself up in the outdoor department, finding a blue tent for ten, a camp stove, staging raids on the food court and the comic book shop, practicing shooting arrows with my mind in preparation for the day Professor X would come to take me to the mansion where I'd find my power and my love. All this was possible in the wide-open newness of a superstore, not in Grady's sticky two-bedroom house with its dirt patch and a pile of busted tires where a yard should have been.

After a few hours of waiting and drawing, I had drifted to sleep on my bed. I heard the door slam, but I knew it wasn't Mama by the way he moved through the house making even the floors and walls sound weak. Grunts and footfalls like a rhinoceros.

"Where's she at?" he asked, pounding his fist on the doorframe.

I wiped the drool from my cheek. "Couldn't tell you."

"You best not lie to me, gal."

I widened my eyes, thinking at him. *I best not? You best not. Throw him against the wall. Throw him against the wall, hard. Throw. Him. Now.*

"You're useless," he said, stepping into the room. "This room was better when I had my weights in here."

Bring the ceiling fan down on his head. Crush his skull. One day, I would not be so small. I bulged my eyes at him.

"Weirdo," he said. "If she comes home, tell her I went out with Mark."

Push their car over the bridge. Into the lake. Block the doors. Puncture the roof.

When Mama got home, her hair was dripping and she

was all keyed up. "Let's go," she said. "We're late." She still had her camera on her shoulder, but there was a crack in the lens cap that wasn't there before. I grabbed my backpack and shoved textbooks and my stuffed dog inside.

"What are you bringing that for?"

"I don't know."

"Please quit fussing over stuff and get in the car. I'll meet you there in a minute. And seat belt, please."

From the front seat of Mama's Saturn, I could see her shadow as she rushed around the house. The mist that hung around all day had finally gathered itself into a solid rain. I always liked the sound of it on the windshield when the car wasn't running. Between the dribbling and the beading and my body heat fogging up the windows, it felt cozy there in the car we'd had since forever.

Pick the car up. Fly the car to Mars. Or maybe California. Maybe I didn't have enough control over my mind's eye to make things happen yet, but I felt like it could happen any day.

"Ready, hon?" she asked. "Let's go see what it's like in a darkroom."

"We're still doing that?"

"Yeah, where did you think we were going?"

"Somewhere better," I said.

"This will be good. I promise. We'll learn something new."

"If you say so."

"Would it kill you to show some enthusiasm?" she asked, with a look on her face that made me wish the camera were blocking it.

"I'm sorry," I said, rolling the window down halfway and back up again so it looked like two separate pieces, two halves operating on their own, the same size and shape, but the lower bit was clear except for the water lines from above. I wondered how many ways I could divide water on that window, thought about folding my notebook paper before starting my drawings, how each panel was its own pod, its own universe.

We drove through the part of town where people had blue tarps over their roofs, car carcasses on blocks, and houses masked by overgrown shrubbery and kudzu. We might have tires, but Grady's house was still in good shape. Least that's what Mama always said when we drove through there. Then she'd be sure to remind me my father lived over here awhile after they separated, but that was the last she'd heard. He hadn't returned her calls when child support came due. I tried to imagine him hunched down under one of the porches like a friendly troll, waiting for me to wander up so he could climb out and shower me with a million un-given kisses, but I knew that sort of fantasy was for babies.

Cave the porch in. Rocks on lumber on body parts.

The art building was empty except for a few straggling painters listening to experimental music that sounded like chainsaws and cracking thunder set to an out-of-tune piano. It was an old building so the music traveled all the way up four flights of stairs to the photo lab, where it bounced around like it was looking for a place to settle.

"Before we go in to process the prints," Caroleen said, "we have to get the film out of the canisters and onto the reels, but the tricky part is, we have to do it in the dark." I tried not to snicker as I followed them into the closet-sized room meant for this sole purpose, wondering how many students had made out in there.

"Okay, do you ladies have your can opener? How 'bout the tank and cap? Scissors?"

"Check, check, and check," Mama said.

"Okay then," Caroleen said, killing the lights. I blinked and stretched my lids and brows wide, trying to ease myself into the blackness. "Pop the lid off the canister and tip the film into your palm. Hold it by the edges." Mama took my hand and put it on top of hers, where I could feel her fingers as she popped the lid. She wound the film around the metal reel, but when Caroleen felt her handiwork, she said it needed to be redone because parts of the film touched.

"What do you think, you want to give it a go?"

"Go ahead, hon. I'm all thumbs. I'll try again on the next one when I've relaxed."

Caroleen found my hands in the dark. "Wipe those off

on your jeans or something. The humidity coming off you will ruin the film."

I waved my hands trying to generate enough air to dry them out and wiped them on my jeans as told.

"That's better," Caroleen said, placing my mother's screw-up in my hand. As I turned the reel, I could smell Mama's dampness and cigarettes and Skin So Soft body oil, orange Tic Tacs and my own Dorito breath. It felt like an hour had passed, but somehow, I managed to loosen and spool the film on the reel and get it closed in the tank without thinking too hard about it.

Mama looked deflated by the time we got the first roll of film processed and hung to dry. "Don't look so glum, Maureen. I screw it up all the time. It's so thin. Do you know how many times I've had the perfect shot scratched all to hell because I was impatient? It's all about control."

"Yeah, yeah. Spare me the pep talk."

"Anyway, we still have printing to do. That's when we get to play. I'm gonna go out for a smoke. When I get back we'll cut the film and put it on the light board. See what's what."

Mama looked through the box of prints that hadn't made the cut, the ones people left behind because they were too dark, washed out from overexposure, had flecks of dust showing, or chemical mistakes. Some were curled around the edges like they'd never had the liquid squeegeed off.

"Wonder why someone didn't like this one?" she asked, pulling a portrait out of the bin.

"I don't know. Maybe she didn't like the way she looked."

"But the lines are nice," she said. "We could do something with the misfits. Make a collage, something."

By the time she pulled a pile of images out, Caroleen was back. She and Mama looked at the negatives on the light board first. When it was my turn, I felt a knot in my throat looking at so many small squares of my face and body with the color inverted. They had already picked the ones they wanted to print so I didn't tell them I'd rather they not print that one in particular. Caroleen set us both up at an enlarger and walked us through what chemical was in what tray, how to agitate, and how long to do it. Mama and I both fell in love with the smell.

After we'd gone through the process with the first few, we took our trays to the whiteboard, where we wiped off the excess liquid. The three of us stood there taking in the newly developed photos without a word. Before long, Mama's eyes turned stony and she walked out. I started to follow, but Caroleen said, "Give her a minute. Stay here and help me clean."

When we got to the car, Mama sat on the hood gazing up at her hands. "Caroleen, may I have a second with my daughter?"

"Sure, hon. I'll turn the radio on. Give you some privacy."

"Come sit by me."

"I'm sorry."

"The way you were looking at me in that photo was like you wanted me dead."

"I don't know what you want me to say, Mom."

"I want you to say you're happy. That I'm imagining hate coming from your eyes."

"I wish we could be somewhere else. Maybe on our own."

"I'm sorry I'm so awful. You don't know what it's like."

I gave her a hug and told her I understood more than she gave me credit for, told her everything would be okay and asked for waffles, so the three of us had a late-night meal, and with full bellies, we dropped Caroleen off at her boyfriend's apartment and drove back to Grady's. Lucky for us, he wasn't home. Mama poked her head in my room after she washed her face, telling me to pack my things if I had anything there worth taking. I didn't lift my pencil from coloring in the gold on Jean's boots, but I nodded, hoping my superpowers had finally revealed themselves, perhaps even been amplified by the film processing room—a room without a speck of light but so full of my mother I almost couldn't breathe.

Fly the car to Mars. Fly the car to Mars. Fly the car to Mars.

WHAT MAGIC

We don't live in the neighborhood anymore. Not where foundations are cracked and the sides of the buildings we called home have already begun their inevitable descent. Where we made games out of which marble—spyglass red or blue—would slide into the left corner of the living room first. Gregg even drew a basketball net, but he couldn't capture the third dimension yet so it looked like a spider web. We don't live where the bugs come in no matter how much poison Mom put out or how much she scoured the place with bleach. Not where cupboards house baggies of flour, of sugar, of coffee and cornmeal zipped up where ants and cockroaches can't get to them. I never told her how I'd pull a stool over to the counter and taste all the spices, how I chewed cloves until the tender parts of my mouth burned and went numb, how the white pepper made me sneeze, how a bug I couldn't name had crawled into the dehydrated onion. Mom must've found it because the next time I was up there, sticking my fingers in Crisco and wondering how she did what magic she did to dumplings and chicken, the onion was gone and everything else was in bags, but no, no. We don't make a special trip to the discount bread store, where we buy six or eight loaves at a time and keep them in the big freezer in the den. We don't cut people's hair in the kitchen anymore, we don't stink up the house with chemicals to make all us bone-tired women look less so. We don't have people banging on the screen door asking for work, asking for money, for a ride, saying "honey, baby please and bless you, child" and stealing our lawn mower once it gets dark because the streetlights haven't blinked on in years. We don't have men standing on porches midwinter in their boxers, smoking and sipping from a brown bag, talking about Texas Hold'em and asking us do we know if our mamas have any cards and pennies because they could show us how to make a living, but no, no. We don't plant vegetable gardens because we need the food. We don't boil cabbage and pressure cook greens, turning the whole house rank. We don't pick chickens clean, or fry livers, patch the backsides and knees of our jeans, brush our teeth with baking soda, or ever hang our wet clothes on the line. And we no longer wait up for Mama to get home from overtime, or stay alone behind locked doors, hiding in the back of the closet, behind coats that smell like stale cigarettes and old fun, our hearts palpitating, sick with solitude come too soon.

GWEN OF ALL GWENS

Gwen lived in a house that was all pitch, eaves, and hard angles. Nights when it wasn't raining too hard, she'd crank the window open in the third-floor loft and climb out, balancing like a dancer, hands and pockets holding a bottle of whatever she could steal: smokes, letters folded into arrows or puzzles or tiny guns, not to mention her own Sharpie and paper. That afternoon, her older brother's bandmate stuck an actual envelope in the pocket of her Army jacket. To gain her nerve, she took a few pulls off the pipe and relaxed her legs over the edge of the roof.

Lately, Amy and Lizzie and Andy picked at her for drifting, for turning sullen, and talked shit about her behind her back for dressing like a "Fleetwood Mac redneck." There was so much in their world she couldn't wrap her head around anymore. Not riding in their cars with the top down, hair tucked into hats, wrapped in scarves, or raging like Medusa in the wind. Not hunting in slinking packs for prom dresses. Not even pilfering overpriced eyeshadow called "snakebite" or "bruise" or "desperation." But more than anything, she could no longer pretend to care about the heft of their thighs or what awful thing David had said after Amy went down on him after months of him pushing. None of Gwen's friends understood the intricacy of her mood and how it had slipped beyond anything she could name. All Gwen knew was it felt good to hang over the edge of high places, to take fire into her lungs, and fucking dare the wickedness to reach her.

She opened the letter and found it full of seeds the size of pinheads, a black leather string snipped from a jacket, and a note written in charcoal on thick watercolor paper.

"Hey, mind if I join you?"

Gwen startled and dropped the paper before she had read it. "Damn it, Chris. Next time you sneak up on me like that, I'm tossing you over."

"I'd like to see you try," he said, pulling himself up and out with a shaking sort of care his sister never had.

"Haven't seen you up here in a while. Haven't seen much of you at all lately."

"I know. Sorry. We're practicing a lot. Supposed to play a show at The Milestone."

"I heard."

"Jason?"

"No."

"Sybil tell you?"

"Don't worry about it. You guys doing flyers?" Chris

cocked his head at her and squinched his lips—confirmation that he knew more than either of them spoke.

"Yeah, thought I'd see if you could make copies if you're gonna be after hours with journalism."

"Sure. You have anything in mind?"

"I don't care. Make it look cool. Graze is opening. The Hellions and Twisted Nipple are playing, too, I think. Get them on there, but we're the headliners."

"A step up."

"Yeah, we're getting better, I think."

It was not so long ago that her brother had slept on her bedroom floor. They'd get high and burn candles and dragon's blood incense and talk until one of them nodded off. If she fell asleep first, he'd return to his room and fall asleep with his headphones on. He knew she got scared at night, despite being too old for such nonsense. What he didn't know was how the fear had become cast-iron, making her wish she could run away from her own body, a little slip of space-time and she'd be back to the decidedly less painful place of matter without consciousness. Gwen picked at the burn scar on her ankle. It was healing, hardening into a strange texture more like vellum. She wished she could peel great swathes of skin off her whole, put them on canvas, make it into a thing that didn't itch, turn herself into mere image, reflection, scrapings of human, but only just. The way she'd felt when the guy had slipped his hand in her pocket. Like the scalding water she'd dribbled from teacup to skin. Like the sky had opened for everyone else and left her on the other side of a kind of glory she couldn't reach and maybe fuck the sky for not letting her in.

"You see Mom before she left?"

"No," Gwen said, lighting two cigarettes at once. "I'm trying something new. Staying out of her way. Hoping not to meet this one. Hoping he'll disappear sooner rather than later."

"I don't know where she finds these guys."

"They find her. They always do."

"You gonna be okay? I have to get to practice."

"I'm fine." She held up her black marker and leaned back against the window, watching the wind pick up, taking the last few leaves off the maple. She drew devil tails, anarchy symbols, "VEGAN" and "GEORGE BUSH SUCKS" in all caps on her white Converse. Filled in negative space with polka dots. When the pipe and pack and bottle were empty, she walked to the edge again. This time she banged her feet on the roofline until she couldn't feel the back of her heels. She peeled off a shingle and sanded the skin off her knee. Nothing. Nothing but restless ache and a hyena inside her she didn't know how to tame. She slid off the roof. She'd done it before.

After her jackknifed breath returned, she found the note in the grass.

The guy had written, "I'm making you something beautiful Gwen of all Gwens," but it was all lowercase and his version of beautiful was missing an 'a' and swirly and smelled of opium oil. On the back, it read in pencil, messy, "Come to the show. —J." It wasn't the first note he'd snuck her. Under her bedroom door while her brother lounged on the sofa watching *Mystery Science Theater 3000*. In her lit book, tucked in between Tolstoy and Wordsworth, which she found when she was writing and rewriting Ophelia's speech, trying to commit it to memory.

By Friday afternoon, Gwen had dyed her hair burgundy. Friday night, she pulled on her jacket, tied the leather string around her wrist, and refolded the smudged note one more time. This time when she slid off the roof, she went looking for him.

Even in the parking lot, the music was loud enough to feel in her lungs.

"I'm on the list."

"Name."

"Gwen."

The bouncer looked at his spiral notebook. "I don't see any Gwen, but you're Chris's little sister, right?"

"That's me. Little sister of all little sisters."

"Damn, girl, if you weren't *his* sister," he said.

"Or fifteen?"

"Or fifteen. Damn," he said, stamping her wrist, straightening himself on the stool.

Across the club, The Hellions high-jumped and screamed at the audience. The crowd circled, hard and fast—a rhythmic fight. Her brother was in the fray, a smear of blood across his cheek. Jason had backed himself against the far wall, pushing people who bumped into him. He studied the guitar player. Gwen wanted to throw her own elbow into Jason's chest to see what he'd do, but she kept her distance and planted herself against the opposite wall. The sweat and pulse of the room moved through her limbs and to her heart to form that same weight that returned again and again at night, whether she was alone or jammed into a club. With a final yelp and a wail of feedback, The Hellions ended their set.

Lights came up and stage smoke sank and stirred as the guys flipped switches and put their instruments away. Band guys always helped each other set up and break down the gear. Sometimes they'd share amps or drum kits to make things easier. Jason nodded at her as he stepped on stage to tell The Hellions, "Killer set, man." She swore she wouldn't get involved with these guys, but this one was persistent and sort of sweet and strange away from the band in the late quiet of her house, with all its hard angles making everything feel more dramatic.

When he strapped his own black Charvel on, he winked

at her. It was then that Gwen knew she'd follow him into some rabid fever dream, their own kind of glory, full of paper guns and ruptured ear drums. As he played, he only looked away from her when it was time to sing backup. She didn't know how to explain to Amy or Lizzie or Andy what she felt being a kid raised by a single mom and the kid of an absent alcoholic, but Jason, he got it. He must have. He lived in a messy trailer about a mile from school with his own single mama.

After the show, she hung around drinking non-alcoholic beer and writing on the club's graffiti-covered walls. In between Antiseen and Bikini Kill and Elevator Action stickers, Gwen drew a dragon with a spiked tail, a bubble circling up above his head: "Our ghetto fortress shall burn forever." As she finished giving the dragon's eyes a little extra black around the edges like the eyeliner-smudged goth boys sometimes did, she felt his sweaty hand reach under her jacket.

"The fuck?" she said.

"You're here."

"You're a genius." She turned out of his attempted embrace. "What do you think of him?"

"Not bad," he said.

"I suppose you could do better."

"No, I'm better with people and scenery."

"I'm not so great with people," she said.

"No, you aren't. For sure."

"I'm not sure what to say to that."

"Well, we're gonna run to try to catch another show at Park Elevator. You coming?"

"Curfew."

"Right. I forget you're younger."

"All the boys do. Anyway, I'd rather beat my mom home so I don't have to see her," she said, lighting a cigarette.

"Maybe I'll convince your brother to stay at home this weekend. We can write songs."

"Maybe you should."

When Gwen got home, her mother's Cutlass was in the driveway. She looked for signs she might not be alone. Movement, shadows against the blinds, music, but she couldn't gather any hard evidence based on the humming porch light and the lamp in the front window. She'd left those on herself. Gwen stood in the front yard, smoking another cigarette, waiting on something she couldn't ascertain. She closed her eyes, thinking of Jason's voice, which, if she was honest, was all the incentive she needed to pursue him. Pain and gentleness and a lifetime of yearning evoked in his regular speaking voice. When he sang? Forget it—she was wet paper. When Gwen opened her eyes, her mother's bedroom light was on so she figured the coast was clear.

She grabbed a few beers out of the fridge and a fudge pop for good measure. In her room, she played one of the tapes Jason had made her and scribbled in her notebook.

Candlelight bounced on her hunter green walls as she tried to imagine being Ophelia herself, pinning poppies in her hair, how sure she was about to be wed in that moment captured on canvas. Gwen rewrote the speech in her notebook for the tenth time. She had to recite it to class on Monday. She had to recite it to herself in her room in an effort to stay her impulses, but her words dissolved into laughter and she drew another dragon instead. This one had eyelashes and her bubble read: "I fell in love at The Ghetto Fortress. How ridiculous."

After she flipped the tape and threw her pillow on the floor, she fell asleep looking at the light shining through the crack under her door. About the time the tape player clicked off, she heard movement downstairs, and soon after, an arrow shushed under the door. Before she could read the note, her mom's bedroom door opened. Woman had some kind of radar where her son was concerned. "Is that my baby?" she called over the landing.

"Me and Jason," he said.

Leave it to her mother to ruin everything. But before long, Jason was strumming his guitar and her mother was cooking something with butter and onions.

Gwen waited as long as she could stand it, but all the crazy shit between her and her mother couldn't squelch her love of her food. When she had her hair braided right, her faded Led Zeppelin T-shirt and shortest sleep shorts on,

Gwen finally left her room. To her surprise, she saw a man in her mother's room, bent over the nightstand. When he stood, he wiped his nose, saying, "Better not say shit."

Jason was at the bottom of the stairwell looking up at her. "What are you doing? I was coming to get you to eat with us. Your mom's made hash browns and is about to fry some bacon." When he saw Gwen's expression, he asked if she was okay, but then she didn't move and her mom's bedroom door slammed, so he headed toward her.

"You look pale. Did you drink too much?" he asked, pulling her down to sit on the top step.

"I'm okay. I only had two beers. I've seen some shit, you know?"

"I hear you," he said, taking her right hand in his. "You see this?" He traced the outline of her palm. "A square."

"I don't understand."

"A square palm means you're restless."

"Didn't I tell you before you were a genius?"

"A square palm also means as a lover, you crave mental stimulation. I can see by your face you're going to throw out the genius line again, but bear with me, Gwen of all Gwens. I see more than you'd like. This, here," he said, sweeping his fingertips across her crosshatched heart line, "means you are controlled but will suffer periods of sorrow."

"Get the guy a MacArthur Fellowship."

"Stop," he said. "Just stop. Come downstairs. I've got a new blue Sharpie with your name on it."

"Thanks, but I can't be around her. Come to my room after everyone's asleep. I'll leave it unlocked."

"Gwen of all Gwens," he said, all throaty and earnest.

And Lord help her after that night, when they would steal away to her bedroom and draw Sharpie tattoos on each other, high on each other's thighs, where no one would see how the devil tails curled.

THE BEST KIND OF LIGHT

When Lorna banged the cat head knocker four times, I knew it was her. Come back after nineteen years. Most women will make their way home if they haven't made something of themselves by the time they're forty, and sure enough, even through the peephole, I could see life had beat my baby down. Damn. And a shirtless kid on her hip, too. I reckon some patterns are passed down in DNA no matter how hard we try to fight the way of it all.

"Mama, come on now. I see you looking. Can we come in or not? I got somebody who wants to meet you."

"I'm coming. I wasn't expecting company." I leaned my weight into the door to wiggle the dead bolt loose. August humidity made the thing swell and I already felt bubbling shame in my throat thinking about all the little house quirks I'd have to explain to Lorna if she was planning on sticking around. The sharp edge on the bath faucet. A junk drawer I can't seem to budge. Towels shoved around the bottom of the washer. Wasp nests in windows. The noticeable slope toward the bedrooms and, hell, half my light bulbs were shot months ago. I make bets with myself on which one's going to bite it next. My coin is on the one in the ceiling fan above my bed.

By the look of Lorna's duffel bag and coffin-sized hard case, it sure looked like all our lives were about to change. She brushed her long bangs out of her eyes with her free hand. "Hey, Mama," she said, putting the child on the ground. With the in-between haircut and plain pants, I couldn't tell if it was a girl or a boy, but the child had big old blue eyes like Lorna's daddy. Downright creepy, if you ask me. She brushed dirt off the seat of the child's pants. "This here is your grandma. Grandma, this is Starla."

"That's a pretty name you got. Like starlight," I said. "The best kind of light, if you ask me." I reached my hand out, but she grabbed hold of Lorna's legs and stuck her thumb in her mouth. "Oh, sorry about that, honey. I ain't used to being around kids. Let me go find an ashtray, get rid of this thing."

"No more coffee can on the porch?" Lorna asked, standing in the doorway.

"I gave up. Keep the living room window raised unless it's raining too hard." I almost asked whether I should move a folding chair and a can back out to the stoop, but it was too early to jump into questions. I dropped it in my half-empty Coke can and tossed it in the garbage.

When I came back, Starla was pawing at her mom to pick her up, but she brushed her off and the child plopped down on the floor, whimpering. Lorna surveyed the living room, but I wouldn't make a statement on what she thought about it, her mouth drooped more now—could be she judged how I was living or could be she was tired. She walked over to the wall where we once kept family pictures. As she ran her fingers through the ends of the macramé wall hanging, I could see she favored one leg and the other was purple at the crease of her knees, but I didn't say a word. Ain't a woman alive who hadn't felt that *putting herself in harm's way* kind of shame.

While she no doubt wondered what happened to the evidence of our lives long boxed up and buried, I grabbed the duffel bag and dragged it down the hall to her bedroom. Lorna followed with the hard case, Starla lagging behind. We heaved the duffel on the bed and Lorna coaxed the zipper open on the overstuffed bag. It looked to be every piece of clothing either of them owned and the whole lot had a dank smell, like laundry dried on a line only to get soaked with rain and thrown in a wet pile on the floor. She pulled out a striped T-shirt and yoga pants.

"The shorts are wearing me at this point," she said, pulling off her belt, showing how poorly they fit. They started to slide off her hips, but she caught them. "Mind if I shower before I do anything? You can keep an eye on Starla, can't you?"

The child appeared in the doorway, sucking both thumbs.

"Sure, we'll be alright, won't we, dollbaby?" She looked up at me like I was a clown coming up out of the woods.

"Baby, this is *my* mama," Lorna said, patting herself on the chest. "She's okay. I'll bet she has some jelly beans to share if you're a good girl."

"I just might." When I stood, the floors creaked under me. Lorna's hair was a lot longer but thinner than the day she left. I tried to imagine all she'd done since the day she loaded up her Jeep. Records and candleholders and skimpy clothes all tossed in banana boxes. A carton of Camels on the seat and a cross hanging from her rearview. "You remember where everything is?"

"Long as you haven't moved anything, I do."

"Very little, Lorna. Very little." I patted her on the shoulder. A soft gesture to let her know I knew what it was like to be out of options. To raise a child you hadn't planned on having. To be world-weary and drawn to cruel men.

She rubbed her face near the spot where the jaw meets skull.

Starla clung to her mother when I headed to the kitchen, but I heard Lorna crouch down, telling her to be brave.

"You'll see," she said. "This is going to be good for both of us. Pinky swear?"

I don't know if the child answered but after the water had been running in the shower a few minutes, she poked her head around the corner. Lorna had dressed her in a Mello Yello shirt, which made her look jaundiced.

"I'm here," she said.

"Me too," I said, pulling a chair out for her. "Now what? I don't have a booster seat."

"I don't need one," she said, climbing up, sitting on her feet.

"They'll go numb with you putting all your weight on them like that. Not that you weigh more than a chicken feather."

"How much does a chicken feather weigh?" she asked, picking at the rubber grapes in the center of the table.

"Can't be more than a quarter of an ounce, but I couldn't say for sure. How about you, dollbaby?"

"I couldn't say for sure, either."

"What can I fix you to eat?"

Starla stuck a rubber grape in her mouth and bit down, the suction making it stick to her tongue. She tried to say *look*, but it came out as unformed noise. I walked over, told her to stick her tongue out again, and plucked it like I would a real grape off a vine, causing her to collapse into a fit of laughter. It took a full minute for her to raise her head from her arms.

"Okay, silly munchkin. What'll it be? Shall I go down the list? What do you like?"

She wiped her nose on her arm and gazed at the figurines in my curio cabinet. "I'm not hungry."

"You got to be hungry. When did you eat last?"

She stood up on the chair, pressing her forehead against the glass. "We had cherry pies from the gas station this morning. They were two for a dollar," she said, trying to see the top shelf on her tippy toes. "What's up there? Can I open it?"

"That's where I keep the most valuable angels. Here, let me show you. Okay if I pick you up?"

The child's curiosity overshadowed her shyness and she reached her arms up. "Now, come on and wrap your legs around me. I'm not as strong as I used to be." I hadn't felt a child in my arms in some time—the feeling caught me by surprise. A soft kind of joy you can't find anywhere else. I grew dizzy with it. I didn't even mind the oily smell of Starla's hair or her sticky-sweet pie breath.

"Why you got so many angels anyway?"

I opened the cabinet for her, realizing it had been a while since I'd dusted. She started to reach for one with its wings folded down and head bowed, but held back.

"It's okay," I said, handing it to her. "I'm not sure. Someone gave me one as a present a long time ago and then seemed like everyone I knew gave me one at Christmas and birthdays. I guess they make me feel better. In a way."

"Why?" she asked.

"I like to think they're looking out for me," I said, touching the figure on the nose. "They're beautiful. The shine of the porcelain, the pastel colors. I like to think about who painted them. I try to remember there's nice things in the world."

"I wish I had wings like her."

"Me, too. Why don't you polish her for me while I fix you some biscuits?"

"Can I?"

"Yes, babydoll. I think she needs someone to look after her. Look how dirty I let her get. I'll get you a rag and a little soapy water."

Starla took her time dipping the rag in the water and washing the angel. She spent the most time on her face and wings. By the time Lorna joined us, I had the biscuits in the oven and fried some bacon. I didn't have much else in the house other than a stack of Lean Cuisines and Boost protein shakes.

"What's with the angel?"

"I figured Starla could take care of her for me."

Lorna stretched her shoulders. "Feels good to get clean. Breakfast for dinner?"

"That okay?"

She nodded. "Baby girl, you ought to feel blessed. Grandma doesn't let anyone touch those angels."

"She sure is pretty," Starla said.

"Not as pretty as you," I said.

It had grown dark out and Lorna reached up to turn the kitchen light on.

"Don't bother. Bulb's out. I can bring a lamp in from the living room."

Her brows pinched and she rubbed her jaw again. "You still got those TV trays?"

"In the garage."

I pulled out a bunch of tea light candles and told Starla to help me set them up on top of the television to give us some extra light. I taught her how to use the point-and-click lighter I kept in case the pilot on the stove went out. Starla placed the angel in the middle, where she could keep an eye on her. Lorna set the trays and carried all our plates to the living room, where we ate in a semicircle around the impromptu shrine, shadows and light doing their dance around the angel while the rest of us tried to figure out how it was gonna be with the three of us under one roof.

A LITTLE ARRHYTHMIC BLIP

No one thought much of Jolene Merriweather until she covered the whole of her wrought-iron fence with silk roses, every one of those suckers wrapped in bright yarn. She had the whole rainbow binding flowers to metal. A body looks on that sort of thing and thinks one of two things: either you think Jolene is a loon or, like me, you see the desperate beauty of the thing—gaps closed with sheer red petals, hands crinkled from unspooling, sore from tying knots—and your own heart sinks with recognition of the spectacle of grief.

Before those manic weeks last fall when Jolene demanded our attention, she'd already captured it. She would come and go from work on foot, a patchwork bag flung across her body, bopping around listening to God-knows-what on headphones too big to stay on her head, as if she were a teenager. The clunky things looked like the kind a large man might have left behind but none of us had ever so much as seen a man at her little corner bungalow. Each morning, she walked out, fresh-faced, eternally clad in mid-length skirts, and disappeared on the horizon, and—as if from ether—

appeared again in the evenings in baggy jeans. Once she closed the door, she only emerged to greet the gal she paid to do her grocery shopping and, on Sundays, to pick dead fronds off her young palm tree.

Jolene had manners, don't get me wrong. She'd wave if we drove past. She'd speak if spoken to, but she never stretched beyond politeness. Some neighbors might have tried to weasel into her life with doughnuts or a box of wine, advice on how to revive her dead lawn, but this lot prides itself on respect for people's privacy. It's her loss if she doesn't participate in the holiday potluck and caroling at Rhoda and Rafi's or the monthly ladies' night at Applebee's. We have fun, we do. But we figured if she wanted to stay all cooped up except to go to work, there must be a good reason for it. I figured it was booze. After a certain hour, a drunk has no time for anything but drinking. She was pretty enough with her thick black braids, but her clothes were well-worn, and, if you looked close enough, you could see her face had the baked quality of earthenware. But I was wrong about the booze. Sometimes, all you see is the past no matter how clear-headed you think you are.

It was late September when things changed at Jolene's—a whisper of a day when we first spent time together. We were having an unusually cool streak and the tops of the maples had begun to redden. It takes a long time for us to get to any kind of autumn down here, so that first day below eighty degrees we were all out planting mums and trimming hedges, pressure washing and painting—all the mundane tasks we tackle when the heat breaks. I bought gardenias to try and tease into a hedge between my house and the Grays' next door. They played heavy metal records until all hours. Early mornings were for spinning raunchy stand-up comedy or classic soul, The Supremes and the like. While they played, the two of them cooked breakfast together, laughing all the while. Frankly, it was more than I could stomach. I hoped a decent boundary might soak up some of the noise. Italian cypress trees were my next step. Tall, fast-growing, and if the wind caught them right, they curled like fingertips. But I hated to get so militant about it. I'd miss the view through their open drapes. Mr. Gray sang to their cats when he thought no one was looking.

I'd taken a break from digging when I saw Jolene come from her shed with a wagon full of fake flowers. The porch chimes jangled sweetly in the breeze, stirring nostalgia for my mother, her Carolina accent, a stack of crêpes slathered in sweet butter, topped with macerated strawberries. Rich and sweet. I massaged the knot in my shoulder, trying my best to feign disinterest, but she looked up from under her flying saucer of a hat to wave me over. I hesitated, looking back at the bushes that still needed planting and the dirt under my nails, but only for a moment. If you want to know an introvert and she waves you over, you go.

The sky was a strange kind of clear—a day with humidity low enough the brilliant light makes your eyes water. A few puffed clouds haunted the horizon. Mist and vapor. Formless and out of reach no matter how much a body longed for such things. Jolene already knelt near the gate with a flower in hand by the time I walked up.

"I see the weather got the best of you, too."

"You ain't lying," she said, waving her flower. "Come on in."

She had on overalls. Hot pink ones with nothing on underneath except a black sports bra. You'd never know we were the same age. Dressing like that always seemed so risky to me. You learn to hide when you're raised by alcoholics. Clothes like that draw attention. I brushed the dirt off my pants as best as I could and hoped she couldn't smell me, regretting the onion I'd added to my tomato sandwich. "Well, Jolene. What is it you've got on the agenda? A little fall decorating?"

"I'm tired of looking at metal," she said, pushing herself up and dropping the flower back in the wagon. "Do you mind helping me with something right quick? I want to use all the hours in the day to put a dent in this project."

"I've got the gardenias to finish."

"It won't take long, I promise. I need another strong back, another set of hands."

"I can't make any promises on the strong bit, but I'm happy to help. What are we dealing with here?"

"Follow me," Jolene said.

Up close, you could see the cracks in the boards, the color the paint used to be in the porch corners—the house needed as much mending as her clothes. But inside, she'd made it her own. The family who owned the house previously had put down wall-to-wall carpet on top of the hardwoods and Jolene had pulled that whole dog- and kid-stained mess up herself. She'd painted the original floors dandelion yellow and put so much varnish on top of them, they shone like the basketball court down at Monroe High. I loved it.

"It's down the hall," she said, folding the brim of her hat up so I could see her face. A little patch of brown pigment on her right cheek suggested a lifetime outdoors. A life of engagement. Of oceanside wonder. Of glittering sand. Fold-out chairs. Hands in dirt. Blooms for days.

Her shoulders were thin and looked to me like it wouldn't take much to make those scapulae of hers meet. I couldn't help but notice them poking out of her overalls. Ever since I learned in high school biology they were also called wing bones, I had tried and failed to make mine sprout. Mostly by contorting my naked body in front of the mirror, trying to get the triangles to touch. Rub them together until you fly. That kind of thing. But a body will look mad to other people, particularly moms who beat you with wine bottles when you're caught acting bizarre. My heart stalled at the thought of it—a little arrhythmic blip that popped up whenever I felt anxious.

"I love your home," I said, taking note of the narrow hallway, the photos of storefronts and big-skied landscapes, dead things on beaches, a puffer fish smiling through death, the friendly eyes not yet cloudy.

"Oh, thanks," she said. "It's small, but it keeps me busy enough, I suppose."

"I envy your style."

"Honey, it ain't much of a style. I'm over here living my dream. When I was a girl, I always imagined heaven must have a floor of pure sunshine, so I painted those beat-up boards yellow. I couldn't afford to refinish them or start over and before I pulled those carpets out, the stink in here would burn your nose clean off your face. Just doing what I can."

"Makes me wish I lived alone."

"It has its perks," she said. "Come on."

I followed her to the only room upstairs, a space made smaller by eaves. The room was warmer than the rest of the house and precious little light came in from a single window at the front of the house. Hunched, Jolene shifted a few plastic containers big enough to hold a body to clear a path to the stairwell. "There," she said, blinking hard and lifting her arm like she was about to sneeze into it. "It's over here."

"Bless you," I said. But the sneeze failed. She wiggled her nose. I walked over and stood on the opposite end of a refrigerator box full of yarn. The lid had been folded into the box and the whole soft mountain of the thing looked like it could come tumbling down at any second. And we were tasked with carting it down narrow steps and out to the front yard. "What's the plan, Jolene? This looks impossible."

"It's not as heavy as it looks, but yeah. I guess I better get some of the ones off the top into bags."

She directed me to the pantry, behind the kitchen, and I disappeared while she started tossing excess yarn toward the stairs. When I returned with two citrus-scented trash bags, she was lying in the box herself.

"I could sleep here and be perfectly content," she said.

"Because that's perfectly reasonable," I said, folding my arms.

"Hey, if I'd wanted a smart ass, I'd have asked one of the girls from the high school for help," she said. "You don't get it. Of all the people in this neighborhood, I thought you'd understand—it's a comfort. If I could knit myself a clone, I would. Let her walk around in the world absorbing all the crap for me without her blood turning cold."

"I suppose it makes a kind of sense. Finding comfort wherever you can." I may not have understood her yarn obsession, but I knew about longing, and as she smiled up at me, I felt a budding kinship. The truth was I found her enchanting. The way she moved. The story of her skin. The house. The giant box of yarn. Cakes and skeins and all.

She pointed her toes, stretching her legs as if she was preparing to dance. "Meredith, can I make a confession?"

"Anything," I said.

"My ass is sinking."

We both burst out laughing, and when I finally regained my composure I said, "That is a pickle."

"I guess we could dig me out."

"Or I could leave. Go back to my gardenias. See how long it takes you to get out on your own."

As I helped get Jolene unstuck, it turned quiet. The air conditioner clicked on. I thought about the last time my husband had joined me in the bathtub. Bubbles spilling over the edge. The tattoo on his chest from his Army days. The ache all the way down to the tip of my fingers. I don't know what Jolene was thinking at the same moment, but it was as though someone had covered us in white sheets. Like unused furniture. When half the yarn lay on the floor, I offered her my hand, steadying my feet into a wide stance for support. She was more frail than she appeared from a distance.

"Well, that'll teach me to lie down in strange places," she said, finally free. "Though you'd think I'd have learned that lesson a long time ago."

"Do any of us ever really learn that one?"

"Maybe not. I'll go get the rest of the trash bags. No point in screwing with the refrigerator box now."

While she was gone, I filled the two bags I'd brought, admiring the names and colors of the yarn. Plum Perfect. Sugar Baby Stripes. Woodlands. Saying these words aloud put me in a better headspace. No wonder Jolene collected the stuff. What would Jack say if I started knitting? Something snarky about embracing my inner grandma, most likely. Would he even look up from his computer long enough to notice? Can a body disintegrate from want?

Jolene returned with trash bags already shaken open and ready. "Let's do this," she said, holding a bag on the ground between her legs, shoveling the yarn into it like she would a pile of leaves.

"Do you do anything like a normal person?"

"What? It goes faster like this," she said, bent over, smiling at me upside down.

"Can I ask you a question?"

"Anything."

I lifted two heavy bags up and over my shoulders. "Where on earth did you get all this yarn? And what in sweet Jesus are you up to?"

Jolene opened her mouth to speak but closed it again. Instead, she got up and walked over to the attic access. The door was child-sized, but she didn't have to reach far for what she was after. She pulled a carved teakwood box out and blew the dust off it. "You try to forget what you've lost. You do everything you know to do. Invent a new person, a new self, a life as different from your old one as you can dream up." She didn't look at me when she handed it over. "But you don't forget. It's nothing but paint over wallpaper."

She removed her hat, scratching at the indentation on her forehead. The brown spot on her cheek seemed darker. "Trade you," she said, nodding at the bags. "I need to get started. I'm burning daylight."

"Okay. Do what you need to do," I said. "Are you sure about this?"

"No," she said, walking away.

I sat with my lap full of her past for eons. I never opened it. I watched shadows. Made shapes in the popcorn ceiling. Counted my breaths. Sat so still my feet went numb below the ankle. I suppose I was waiting for her to come back. I suppose I hoped if I sat there long enough I would atomize. Or astral project. Figure out a way to dip under one of the millions of gravitational waves and live parallel to whatever this place had become for me. And Jolene. And the rest of us ghost people. But amid my drifting, Jolene began to sing something ancient and Gaelic, her voice capable of lower tones than I'd have thought. The timbre of loss coming not from her throat, but deep in the diaphragm. Roused, I gathered four bags and met her out front, where she'd already wrapped several flowers to the left of the gate.

"We'll do the gate last," she said.

I lay my hand on her head. Her hair so much finer and smoother than my own. "I have to go. The gardenias."

"Oh, okay," she said, without looking up.

"I'm sorry."

"Don't be, silly. Come back anytime."

October came and went. We all watched Jolene work from behind closed doors, from stoops and sidewalks, talking amongst ourselves about what it could mean. Rhoda begged me to tell her what her house was like inside, but I was unwavering in my silence on the matter. Something changed in me once I'd spent some time with her. She needed whatever protection I had to offer. By November, when sunny days were rare, she had finished everything but the gate. We hadn't talked again. She'd waved a few times and I nodded back. Jack asked me what happened over there, but I wouldn't tell him anything beyond the tangible. I helped her carry a shit ton of yarn down to the yard. "You can see the truth of it yourself. The evidence is on her fence for heaven's sake," I said.

"I know what I know," he said. "You're different since that day."

"Maybe it's you who's changed."

"I know what I know," he said.

It was a Sunday when she got to the gate. A warm, dark

morning, but the weather called for drastic temperature drops and a fifty percent chance of freezing rain overnight. I covered my gardenias even though Jack said it was unnecessary. Jolene came out in her pajamas and fox head slippers, one last bag at her side, and set to work. This time, I walked over uninvited. "Morning," I said.

"Yeah," she said. "It is."

"Need some help? It's supposed to get cold."

"No, I'm all set," she said.

Up close, the fence was breathtaking even on a day when thick cloud cover muted the color in everything. Sugar Baby Stripes. Woodlands. Perfect Plum. The memory of Jolene's cackle as she sank in the refrigerator box six weeks earlier. She worked silently, braiding red, yellow, and orange together, wrapping it around another flower, and another, and another. I knelt on the other side of the gate. "I'm sorry."

She took a deep breath and finally looked me in the eye. Those dark eyes like a priest's. The splotch on her cheek, lighter. Her chin, pink with emotion. "What kind of person are you?" she asked.

"The kind who runs," I said.

"No. I don't believe that's true." She looked back down at her work, started moving her hands again. Her knuckles had swollen in the past few weeks. She had new scars and hangnails. "I'm the runner of this little duo," she said, sliding the lock on the gate.

I joined her on the other side. Scooping up a lapful of roses, I asked what she wanted me to do.

"Tell me the truth," she said.

I handed her rose after rose. Picked out yarn colors: Starlet Sparkle. Sea Fret. Boho. Darling and Archangel. The air chilled. I pulled my cardigan tight, but it wasn't enough. I wondered how long it would take to wrap me in Archangel, which you wouldn't imagine by the name but was in fact a scrumptious, albeit mellow, variegated pink and purple.

Several hours passed. We had almost closed every remaining gap in the gate. Jolene sang more of her Gaelic songs that I imagine had lyrics about heart love and dead children and harvest moons. When she stopped singing, she said again, "Tell me the truth."

"About what?"

"Anything," she said.

"I didn't open the box from the attic."

"Why not?"

"I didn't have to."

"You think you have me figured out, then?"

"Those aren't the right words."

"Is there any more Archangel? I think I want to finish with that."

"I think I mean I didn't want to know. Whatever you lost."

"Whomever."

"Yes, whomever."

"Because you lost someone, too."

"Yes."

"Tell me the truth," she said again. "You can't be a part of this project unless you speak truth. What kind of person are you?"

"I'm the kind of person who withdraws. I've buried too many people. Jack doesn't love me anymore. I resent him for not wanting children. I don't want to let go."

"Maybe you won't have to."

"I always have to."

"Yes," she said, tightening the loops around the bar she worked on. "Where are we on that Archangel?"

"Fresh out."

"Fresh out of Archangel," she repeated. "They're never around when you need them, are they? I suppose I'll settle for Emerald City."

And so, Jolene wrapped the rest of the gate, spikes and all, with an eye-blasting green, which seemed completely off compared to the colors leading up to it, but who was I to judge. It wasn't my place. Or my project. Or my grief. She did what she needed to do. When she finished, she put her hands on her hips and turned counterclockwise to survey all she had accomplished. I have no way of knowing what she was thinking in that moment, but I imagine our minds wandered parallel universes. Ones in which we were still alive, despite everything. And maybe, just maybe, we could come back to the present. Allow ourselves to be vulnerable enough to become old friends.

She bent down to the ground, still warm from where we'd been working, and wiped the dew from a few blades of grass. When she turned to face me, she smeared the dew across each of my cheekbones and then fell to her knees. She repeated the motion, this time marking her own face. I knelt next to her, the moisture tingling on my cheeks, and from my throat a single call—*war paint*.

FOR A BLAZE OF SIGHT

after Muriel Rukeyser

My whole world consists of warm pine and honeysuckle when I'm splayed out on the grass. The fragrance used to be a comfort, as did morning light on my cheeks, but as spring comes now, a humming dread rolls in with it. A sickness at the thought of sweat. A pulse behind my eye with the thousand tiny ways the warm seasons remind me of all that's lost. Dandelion fluff can't be disassociated from Nicole's hands. The sound of kids' feet hitting pavement, jumping double Dutch. Unfurling leaves take me back to my long-distance running days, when I could drop down off curbs and hoof it up flights of stairs without a care— bass drums thumping, feminist playlists telling me to shake it off, shake it out, fill it with rage—my heart rate steady, headphones causing my ear canals to ache. Now, lines of perspiration forming where my thighs meet my pelvis trip the alarm set deep in my nervous system.

Some events are asteroids. The debris, unshakable.

It's nearly three years since I lost the eye. I miss the fleck of brown outside my iris. Steven agreed it was a shame to lose the right and not the left, since the left is so dreadfully ordinary. He didn't say it, mind you, he gave up after months of my badgering him about it—his cheeks slackening the moment he could no longer pretend. I often wonder if that eensy splotch on my right eye made me the person I was before. A woman capable. A woman grace-built with long limbs and lashes full enough to brush the lenses of heart-shaped sunglasses. Feminine sweet. Perhaps even tender. Had Nicole survived, things might be different. Normal, even. She'd help me forget about my eye, and we'd keep our catalogue shopping and wine Wednesdays, and maybe one day we would share coffee and huddle together at the bus stop, sending our big girls off for the day, getting lost in the detritus of school projects, construction paper and poster board, rubber cement and glitter, so much glitter. But when I woke from the accident, they told me about Nicole first, my eye second. So here I am without my Irish twin, stretched out on the ground, counting the days until the three-year mark, hoping once it's past, I can catch my breath again.

I can live. Or I can die.

One hundred and fifty-three Sundays since I lost half my sight, half of a life shared. As I said, I still like to lie in the yard like I did in the thickest fog of grief—those brutal recovery months—each day a lifetime and a fraction of a second distilled—every moment defined by its movement away from the event. In the beginning, when I was still bandaged and desperate to get a handle on gravity, bumping into everything, with the purple knees to show for it, I got the idea to flatten our pristine HOA-required fescue grass into shapes like croppies do in great wheat fields.

I don't know what made me do it that first time. Except to say it's something when half your world goes black. I suppose it was related to insomnia and grief or vertigo and hours upon hours of documentaries on all manner of strange and unusual happenings. The fire in the Chicago theater. Thermite and the Hindenburg. Angry ephemera at the rifle manufacturer. The bile-inducing wave of riled-up white supremacists in Oregon after US Marshals shot a "survivalist's" son and wife. Pet food industries poisoning our animals. The inevitability of a factory farming–spawned virus that'll kill us all. But then in the witching hour, when I was half-covered in cheese curl dust and unable to locate hope outside a full wine bottle, I caught a film about an elderly Englishman who took visible joy in listening to what wheat and long grass said, how he never meant to cause hubbub about aliens. "It's something there, speaking," he said, puffing on his pipe. "Mother Earth. She murmurs. One only has to listen hard enough." I wanted to hear what he heard. When the show was over and the infomercial about wrapping yourself skinny started, I switched the television off. The sun hadn't quite risen, but I felt my way down the safety rail on our deck until my feet touched grass. When I lay down, disoriented and reeling from trying to adjust to a flat world where all color seems wrong, I called out to the unseen. Not too loud, mind you. A little hum—a melody stuck in my head. I lay there night after night, snuggled into the grass Steven was no longer allowed to mow until something finally popped in my head—not a sound, but an image, a pattern I couldn't shake.

On my first attempts, I fell down a lot and the designs looked like nothing. Rumpled grass after a picnic. The truth is I don't think the earth spoke to me the way she did to the Englishman. But I kept at it, put the baby in the middle of the yard in her empty yellow wading pool. She was my reference point—her fat rolls a reason to live. She wasn't quite crawling but would play with her busy station, making itty-bitty tings and giggling until she wore herself out and curled up with her stuffed lion, sweat dampening her baby fuzz. After an hour or so, I'd tire out, too, and try not to look at myself in the fake mirror when I picked her up.

"Mommy's losing it, sweetie," I'd whisper into her elbows and the backs of her knees. "But Mommy loves you." And when I pulled back, "Not everyone can say their Mommy does, mind you." But there was something to it, some tiny vibration in the earth, and it grew with each attempt. I miss this time with Anna. She's old enough now to run away from me, knows I can't chase her without losing my balance and cackles at me from behind the weeping willow. I try not to dread the day she realizes other moms have two eyes and stereoscopic vision. I try not to imagine her face one day when her cousin tells her I caused the crash or what it'll do to their friendship. I try not to think about her grandmother phoning Steven, asking him to bring her to the farm to visit, or his nail-picking when he told me.

"I know it's tough," he said, looking at the floor. "But Anna needs her grandmother."

"Too bad your mother's gone," I said.

"I don't know that she'd have been any better, but yes, it breaks my stupid heart she didn't have the chance to meet Anna. Your mom—I'm not sure it's fair to keep them apart."

"You've made your choice. I don't know why you—you made it months ago. I don't know why you're looking to me for permission. Pick her. Queen mother. Everyone does."

"It doesn't have to be like this, Jane," he said, brushing his hair out of his eyes. "It's not so bad. She's not. Besides, I'm not picking her. I'm putting our daughter's needs ahead of our own."

"Take her and go. Live there. I could give a shit."

Steven looked at me like I had ripped off my own scalp, threw it at him, and had it in me to do the same to him. What can I say? It's when you are most desperate for connection that you shove it away, hard and fast, a bloody projectile hurtling into oblivion. It's a miracle he didn't leave.

I'd like to say my behavior has improved since then, but I've seen that same bewildered look so much I'm almost disappointed when I lash out and get calm mouths and healing caresses from the wide world of the concerned.

After three years of flattening shapes into our grass and letting it grow long again, I've learned to sketch first, to create small daily goals. I've found it's best to move counterclockwise, to follow my good eye. My favorite tools are my bare feet. With them, I tramp pears and droplets and bisecting lines, feeling the weather in my toes, the microcosm of living things tickling my arches, how the trees talk to each other through their root systems long after one of their own has fallen. Recently, I moved on to more complicated spiral patterns, my nod to the extinct ammonites, relatives to squid and cuttlefish and octopus, who are reproducing at alarming rates in our warming oceans. I like to imagine great swarms of them in epic love throes. Tentacles and legs everywhere, blocking out the refracted light fifty feet below the water's surface.

My designs improved when I started tying a three-foot length of rope between my ankles and stopped drinking as much. It's progress, sure, but lying here, my visual of how pear blossoms fall still makes me blue—forever stretched and warped and pushed off-center. Resting my head on my arms, I let them brush over me. For a few moments, I soften to wonderment, wishing I could transform into a lusty sea creature, hell-bent on sex and death. Though I'd closed my eye, I felt Steven standing behind me. Light and heat disappeared. His body blocking my sun. Not sure if I was sleeping or awake, he stayed put for a few minutes, shifting his weight from left to right, clicking the grill tongs in series of threes. Eventually, the sun returned and the screen door screeched shut. After three years, the poor guy lost his ability to speak to me about anything but food and physical symptoms. His fidgeting silence was a clear signal he was close to giving up. I wished he would.

I wanted the spent blooms to accumulate in the rivet where my eye used to be so I could pack them tight—like a nurse armed with gauze. Tamp the petals down to encourage germination so I may sprout into a sapling. I could become a light sweetness on the air no one could name if I fixed myself there next to the weeping willow, learning to bend and sway, to shed my leaves in autumn. Or perhaps once the tender skin is covered, I would heal. I could catch Anna and swing her in circles until we fell in a fit of giggles. I'd try my hand at cartwheels. Because the recurring dream where the world swooshes by as I careen head over feet on mother's front lawn was becoming too much to bear. Green over blue, of the earth, of the sky, until I woke with vertigo. The oils might've lingered on my skin, but the blooms would loosen, blow away, and disintegrate like everything else. Transformation was foolish, impossible.

Petals slid down my cheekbone. Pink-tipped renegades landed on my shoulder, telling me the sun had baked my skin too long. Of the earth, by the earth. Steven would never understand. If I spoke these thoughts, he'd look at me sweet and place an overfilled plate of barbecue chicken on my lap, telling me all I needed to do was eat. "You'll feel better," he'd say. "It doesn't have to be so hard, this life. You got to get some protein in you. Got a good glaze on it this time. Same way you used to."

I wiped myself off and went inside, where he was already seated. Sure enough a plate of chicken thighs and burnt dogs waited next to fruit salad and peas. Anna reached for our blue whale butter dish, but Steven was an expert at deflecting her little arms with his elbow while scraping the last bits of food off his plate.

"Hi, Mommy," he said. "We've done well with our sweet peas. We're so proud, aren't we?"

"We are," I said, moving my plate closer to the food so I could hold it and the serving dishes. You have to hold on to things when you lose an eye, or you misjudge, grab empty space, your hands thudding against tabletops. I retrieved a chicken thigh and a hot dog with my fingers, licking the juice off before I grabbed tongs for the fruit. Peas are difficult without a spoon and a bowl unless I eat them like Anna does, chasing one at a time around the plate. Steven forgot but realized his mistake when I sat down without them. "Don't worry about it," I said. "But if you wouldn't mind putting some ketchup on my dog, I'll give you a million dollars."

"What I could do with a cool million," he said, leaning toward Anna. "Swimming pools and movie stars."

I tried not to focus on his face anymore, to let it soften into a haze like everything else. A woman can only take so much forced effort, so much pity, such worried brows and clenched jaws. If he and I could unlearn the things our bodies do when our mouths stay shut, perhaps we could make it. He shook the container on his way over and squeezed a dollop onto my dog, but the bottle splurted and ketchup landed on my pineapple. "Don't worry about it," I said.

Anna banged on her tray, pea mush still on her chin. He didn't clean her up fast enough. He didn't, he didn't, he doesn't. When Nicole was still alive (therapist that she was even during off hours and despite being my sister and most definitely the last person I would ever hire in that capacity), she used to try to shift my negative thinking. I never realized how much so until she was gone. "Yes, but Jane," she would've said, "Look at the way he cradles her. Not many fathers dote that way. Ours sure as shit didn't. He plays with her. How come you don't recognize all the light there?"

I'm not sure we'd have stayed married this long without her behind-the-scenes assistance. But I was the problem all along. Not Steven.

"I appreciate you fixing dinner," I said. "Chicken's good. Juicy."

His eyes crinkled at the hint of a smile. "How's it going out there?' he asked, wiping Anna's face with his own stained napkin.

"You know I hate it when you ask me that."

"Is there a better way to say it?"

"I don't know."

"Anna Anna Bo Banna," he sang, scooping her out of her chair.

"It feels like you're judging me."

"I know. You've said so before, but I think you're—what would Nicole say? Projecting."

"Please don't."

"I'm sorry," he said, making googly eyes at our daughter. "It's time for someone's bath anyway." He balanced Anna on his hip and two plates and her sippy cup in the other hand. Her legs dangled, looking longer all the time. I crumpled my napkin and tossed it too far right of the plate. A dragonfly knocked into the bay window. I never felt more childish or sick of him being the decent guy.

I cleared the table though it took me longer to balance my plate and the leftovers. It took four trips between the dining room and the kitchen, the door swinging back and forth between. My speed got ahead of me. When I turned around too quickly, trails followed like tendrils trying to pull me back to the earth. I wrapped the bowls and stacked them too high in the fridge, but the food was put away. Upstairs, the tub was filling and the two of them sang her bath time song. The hot pink Tyrannosaurus rex would be splashing in the ocean before long. God help buzz-cut Barbie.

When the kitchen was half as clean as Steven would like, I headed toward the back door, but when I reached for the handle, I turned and went upstairs to my family, rolling my sleeves up when I got to the bathroom.

"Look who's here," Steven said, keeping his eyes on Anna as he pushed her chin up with two fingers, pouring water over her hair from a half-empty Barrel of Monkeys.

"Save some water for the bath, for goodness' sake," I said, splashing my way inside.

"It couldn't be helped. There was a dinosaur-induced earthquake."

"And a tsunami followed?"

"Precisely," he said, scooting over enough for me to squeeze in.

"Well, we better get buzz-cut Barbie to safety. Looks like it's too late for the monkeys," I said, pointing to the red plastic figures covering the drain.

"I'm afraid so." He poured more water over Anna's shoulders. "What do you think, little missy? Yes. They're a goner. And Barbie?" Anna hid her behind her back and leaned against the edge of the tub, laughing like a maniac.

"I'll save them," I said, picking out one at a time, hoping their curled arms would loop. "Look, look. This guy's saving his friend." I dangled the pair over Anna's hands and she was so thrilled she leaned forward, clapping and splashing, and buzz-cut Barbie bobbed up to the surface. We were soaked. "I'll get some more towels, Papa."

"That's nice to hear," Steven said.

"Towels?"

"Papa."

I returned with more towels than we needed, trying not to think of an elaborate fractal, petal upon petal upon petal—the way a flower looks like a fist before it opens and how it must go on for eternity under a microscope. Tossing them at Steven, I tried to get another laugh, but the tone had shifted and Anna started crying because she wasn't ready to get out.

"But sugar lump, your little fingers are so wrinkled," he said, pulling a towel around her shoulders. "Looks like b-e-d-time is going to be fun tonight." He took a deep breath and tossed her over his shoulder, trying to get her back to silly, but it didn't work. Her lip quivered. Her thumb went in her mouth and the tears fell almost immediately. It's like there was a direct link between thumb and tear ducts, but this kind of crying was manageable. She'd be asleep as soon as we got her dressed and tucked in. Buzz-cut Barbie, T-rex, and the monkeys stayed in the tub.

Sure enough, she was out in five minutes, her little lip still moving as she nursed her thumb even in her sleep. Steven pulled the cord on the cupcake-shaped lantern in the corner, letting out a deep sigh. His back cracked as he leaned into side stretches. Under faintly purple light, he said again, "Nice."

"I know," I said, walking up behind him and hooking my arms under his and around his broad chest. I lay my head against his shoulder blade, turning so my good eye was covered and the room went black. For a moment, we were only damp clothes and warm bodies, the scent of baby shampoo hovering.

"Maybe you're right."

"About?"

"My mother." He turned around, put his hands on my waist like we were at a middle school dance. For a moment, it felt like he might sing or twirl me, but instead, he smoothed my hair out of my face, and even in the dim light, I felt his pity return as he took a step back.

"I can call her, then? That would be so great. I think she could do some good."

I wanted to tell him I knew it wasn't only about Anna. He hoped Mother and I would fix our shit. He hoped when we did, it would mean I was fixed. We could put this whole unfortunate incident behind us and get back to normal. I wanted to tell him to get fucked, that he could leave, take

Anna if he must, that I'd be fine. Life would go on. But I couldn't. I would never be fine. So, with only his speck of hope between us, I gave in. "Okay."

It took a few months of back and forth and rescheduling, but we finally agreed on a day to visit and stuck to it. The night before, I woke barely an hour into sleep. I had one of those nightmares you know is recurring while you're dreaming, but when you're conscious all you remember are flashes, dogs you've loved and lost covered in blood, something horrible you're trying to protect them from, a falling, a fire. Nothing. My heart pounded in my ears, sounding like that first ultrasound before we knew Anna was a girl— the beating, all liquid. I couldn't shake the thought of sea creatures, how we all emerged from salt water, from bacteria, from scale and fin. My mother teaching Nicole and me how to gut a fish. How she'd wrap the innards in paper grocery bags with spent lemon rinds to try to curb the smell. How her hands looked thin-skinned when she was a decade younger than me. What she'd say to me when we visited when I hadn't been able to face her since the accident. I'd heard she'd gone back to drinking. That she was thinking of selling the farm, moving into town. That her hips were shot.

Steven let me sleep late. When I finally went down, he slid a coffee across the bar like we were at a saloon, tossed the kitchen towel over his shoulder, and leaned on the counter. "How are you feeling this morning, gorgeous?"

"Okay," I said, slurping down half the cup of coffee. "What's all this?"

"Breakfast of champions," he said, turning back to flip a pancake.

"That's a lot of food."

"I thought we should fuel up before our road trip."

"Jesus. Already?"

"I called her as soon as I got up."

"And?"

"Didn't cancel. Said she'd have supper waiting."

"I don't know, Steven." I slid my coffee back to him for a refill. "I don't think I can face her."

"It'll be good. I know it. Now, do you want butter or chocolate and whipped cream like me and baby girl?"

"Just butter. Anna in the living room?"

"Yes, she and half her stuffed animals are watching a movie. Go join her and I'll bring in the food. We'll have a picnic. A pancake picnic and a road trip. The perfect Sunday."

"If you say so."

I curled up with Anna and her menagerie of fuzzy critters she'd arranged in a half-moon around the television. She used the biggest one—a white bear she'd named Sugar—as a pillow and snuggled as many as she could under her Wonder Woman blanket. She must've been up for hours to be so calm. She patted my knee and leaned into my side until Steven came in with his breakfast masterpiece. Her eyes had never seen such glory outside the pancake house. We rarely gave her so much sugar. I wondered if getting her hopped up before strapping her into a car seat for four hours was a good move, but I didn't want to spoil the moment. Their eyes said cheers to each other in that exclusive papa-daughter way.

As we ate, I constructed a new piece, a horseshoe crab, one of the oldest species on the planet. Not a fractal or a traditional shape for a crop circle, but a marvel of a creature. Two compound lateral eyes. One thousand ommatidia. More eyes that detect visible and ultraviolet light. More eyes on top. Ventral eyes near the mouth. Photoreceptors. The biggest rods and cones of any known animal, and they still have relatively poor eyesight but are more sensitive to light at night and tied to circadian rhythms; between that and their blue blood, medical researchers have a field day with the poor suckers. The horseshoe crab was an obvious choice for my totem. I loved the thought of an entire seabed crawling with them, powered by moonlight, feeding on mollusks.

In the car, I pulled my shades on and my ball cap down. Anna sang made-up songs about butterflies and sunbeams and pine trees until she fell asleep. Steven put on a playlist he'd made for the trip. Songs that made me tuck my knees into my chest. Van Morrison, for one. The last time I danced to that song was not with Steven but with Nicole. He should remember. He was there, for fuck's sake. Fourth of July the year I was pregnant with Anna. Her daughter

Sadie, six months old and sleeping, swaddled in a bassinet in the living room. Nicole came out after checking on her with a fresh beer and her ponytail tied with red and white string. "What happened to the blue?" I asked. She'd run out of time trying to make it back before the fireworks started. "I didn't know it'd take so long to get it wrapped," she giggled, shaking her head so hard the red and white strands whipped us both face to face, almost forehead to forehead. Our bare feet muddy from the sprinklers, we spun like we did when we were girls until we fell ass-down in the melodious glop of a summer night. She lay her hands on my belly and sang to Anna, messing up all the lyrics. She was high on kind bud and I was drunk on my own cocktail of baby anticipation, sister love, and early seventies rock.

"Why'd you put this on the playlist?"

"You're smiling, aren't you?"

"Until I'm not."

"But, baby, shouldn't it be about the smile and not what comes after?"

"Said the man who's never killed anyone."

"It's such a nice memory though."

"I'm done trying to explain it to you. Can't you put on talk radio?"

He turned the music off but didn't bother with anything else, so we spent the remainder of the ride in silence. I couldn't shake the flurry of images between that July night and the night of the accident. A brutal flipping of pages between a dance and blood and glass and Nicole's legs twisted unnaturally beneath her, stuck, nearly chin to chin, but inside a funnel of darkness. When we pulled up the long, gravel drive, Mother was standing on the porch, a kitchen towel in her hand.

"Maybe this wasn't such a good idea," I said, biting the inside of my cheek.

"She'll be glad to see you, I promise. She's missed you. Everyone knows the accident wasn't your fault."

"At least we can shove Anna in her arms. That ought to make her happy."

"Babe," he said, unfastening his seat belt. "Do you hear yourself?"

"What?" I said. "It's the truth. You don't know her like I do."

He let out a deep sigh. "I'll get Anna up. Go say hello, for God's sake."

Walking up to the porch, I noticed she'd had the tulip tree cut down and the split rail replaced with chain-link. Acres of corn grew behind the house, the bright green stalks swaying in the late afternoon sun. A pair of goats stood on a picnic table no human had used for years, their ears flicking at my approach. I tried to go down the animal classifications, to count the spaces between the invertebrate horseshoe crab and the mammals before me, but I didn't know much about goats aside from a reputation for destruction and fainting. Mama's hair was longer than it had been since me and Nicole were children. A small clump of curl caught the breeze, tapping against her shoulder.

"Hey, Mama."

"Hey, baby," she said. "Get on up here so I can get a look at you."

"I'm here."

The slats creaked as I stepped onto the porch.

"If that don't beat all," she said. "Never thought I'd have a one-eyed kid."

"I never thought a lot of things." I said.

She held me at arm's length and examined me hard. "You look like hell, gal. And skinny. Too damn skinny. But then Nicole was always the better eater."

The woman had a way of usurping all my words. I stood there, mind racing, but my mouth frozen into, according to Steven, a grimace.

"Mrs. Shirley?" he called, breaking the often-seen, rarely mimicked, mother-daughter shit spell. "Anna here told me she was hungry."

"Give me that baby," she said, transformed. She held Anna's head to her chest and smooched her forehead until Anna broke out laughing. Mama booped her on the nose and lowered her to the ground, first swinging her between her legs like she'd done a thousand times with my sister and me. "Let's eat. I made stew beef and macaroni and cheese."

Steven started to make a face at me, but I shook my head no.

I didn't say much over lunch, but Mama was happy to see me eat for once. She kept on and on about Nicole's appetite, how healthy she'd always been, what a good attitude she had about her body. But I suppose it would appear that way to someone who never had to clean her up after she vomited in the bathroom of damn near every restaurant she'd ever been in. Anna didn't like her stew, had, like me, never been a fan of meat, but thankfully Mama didn't pay much attention. Steven went for the antacids in my purse the first chance he got. I smelled the chalky mint on his breath when he returned to clear the table after he laid Anna down for her nap.

"How long y'all staying?"

"You tell me. Wasn't this your and Steven's master plan?"

"I was gonna can some corn tomorrow. Got four bushels and more coming."

"Put us to work," Steven said.

"What is Anna going to do if we're in the kitchen all day?"

"We can teach her a skill," Mama said.

"Lord, Mama. She's too little."

"Well, she can watch television or play outside, then."

"On her own? That defeats the whole purpose of our visit, does it not?"

She broadened herself, the way she had always done when she was angry, like she'd been walking around as two-thirds of herself and all of a sudden there she was, larger than life and full of poison.

Turning her back on me, she spoke directly to Steven. "And what is it my only living child wants to do while she graces me with her presence? Perhaps you can enlighten me?"

"I'm sorry, Mrs. Shirley. We only—"

"Steven," I said, placing my hand on his chest. "There's no need. Go check on Anna. I'll be up shortly." Without hesitation, he scooted away. Though it had been years, Steven had witnessed Mama's handiwork before. There's nothing quite like the anger of a woman who feels she never got her due. Particularly from her children. Particularly from the survivor.

Mama stood her ground, but I did not engage the way she wanted. I would not raise my voice. I would not beg her to love her grandchild. I would not explain myself. This was a woman who rose at daylight and bedded down at dusk, a woman who had given birth, both times in her own bed. We spoke different languages. And our translator was gone, dead going on three years. Instead, I walked out the back door, kicking my shoes off before I entered that glorious field of green.

For a while, she watched me from the window, a shadow against the incandescent glow of her kitchen. A light she never turned off. But eventually the shadow disappeared. The moon moved across the sky as I worked felling cornstalk after cornstalk without much thought. A hawk squealed in the distance and sometime later swooped near me with a squirrel in its talons, still trying to wiggle away. At some point, a thorn had lodged itself in my pinky toe, and my lower legs were bruised like hell, but I kept at it until the sky began to lighten again. As I neared the center of my crab creation, I liked to think I was making a thousand rudimentary eyes, but how do you translate such a thing to other people? They may never know what I'm trying to say is *here—here is what's left of me. Light receptors. Circadian rhythms. Muddy feet.*

STILL SOFT, STILL WHOLE

I wore Stargazer lilies in my hair the day me and Beau got married. Dee had separated my hair into six ponytails, three on each side of the part right down the middle. I remember saying maybe we should leave it, that way my hair would look as wonky as I felt. But she twisted each set of three together and fastened them under the opposite ear. It was so tight I thought it must've taken a couple years off the worry lines on my forehead. But then she tucked the lilies in and I stared at a pretty little creature in the mirror I didn't hardly recognize. The glitter. The makeup. It was all too much.

"All you're missing is your wings," Dee said.

When I baby-stepped it down the aisle in my mermaid dress, I tried to focus on sweet Beau's green eyes and long lashes, what we'd done in the back of my truck two nights back, Taylor Swift playing on the radio, the chilled wind on my knees. But my hair was a halo of smells reminding me of Daddy's midsummer funeral. Sprays of lilies wilting in the heat and all of us hungover from sitting up with him in Mama's front parlor. Daddy was a fighting mixture born to

Irish immigrants who'd settled in Appalachia. All of them washed in the blood of the lamb and whatnot. Worn out hymnals and a hand-me-down King James. Jesus's words in red. It might seem weird to outsiders to have a wake in the house, but Daddy wanted what Daddy wanted. Wrote it down. Had it notarized. "Put the coffin next to the piano. You might have to move it to the right a tad, but it'll fit." I measured the thing myself. I should have known it would all go to hell because when me and Beau were lighting our eternal flame candle, all I could think of was Daddy's waxen fingers and the smudgy rouge on his dead cheeks.

Me and Beau had a quick courtship. Not a year after Daddy died, my previous sweetheart fell for my sister. He and Dee ran off to Los Angeles, the city she described "like warm watery light but you know, not afraid to get down and dirty either." She liked the grime. "Nobody wants to be a damn saint," she said. Long as she stayed home, wasn't nothing else she could be, and Charlie, he understood. She figured that's why they was meant to be. Fated. It bothered me more that Dee had found her ticket out than the sticky circumstances of her departure with my boyfriend. Charlie didn't do much for me anyhow. Those overlapping front teeth of his would've driven me away in the long run. He didn't say much the day he came for his things, but I put my hand on his shoulder, wished him well, and asked him if he knew what he was getting himself into. With Dee. With

Los Angeles. The fatalism running through both. As he packed, I turned the word *underbelly* over and over in my mind, but kept it to myself. Charlie's little paunch. A cluster of scars on his hip from road rash. The half-rancid smell of the pomade he used to slick his hair back. His affection for brown liquor. He turned his head as he wrapped his electric toothbrush in bubble wrap, "I can't help myself. I reckon it'll end in tears, but I got to see it through." And ain't that the way of it for most of us? I met Beau a week later at Home Depot buying annuals for my flower beds.

I'd already loaded up two bags of mushroom compost and two bags of organic topsoil on my pallet and pulled the orange thing behind me up and down the aisles, the sun hot on my head. Dark-headed people know what I'm talking about. A hundred scalp burns in a lifetime. I'd stopped in front of a pot of pink and purple hyacinths. I closed my eyes, taking a deep breath through my nose, savoring the heavy perfume in the air that took me back to my parents' house in March. Muddy and gray save for the splash of color and sweetness from Mama's bulbs. "We may not have much," she'd say, "but that don't mean we can't make what we got pretty."

"I hate to tell you, but it's too late to plant hyacinth. The blooms will be spent in a week and you'll have to wait a year to see your handiwork," a man said too close to my ear. The prickles started along my neck and traveled. Shoulder. Valley. Rib cage. Like a fuzzy caterpillar crawling right down into my heart, and I hadn't even turned around yet.

Of course, I jumped back and knocked my elbow on the pallet handle, so the first words out of my mouth to this pretty man were, "Son of a bitch."

He laughed. "So sorry, hon. Didn't mean to scare you. Here, let me see how bad it is." He cradled my arm in his hand, turning it this way and that. The heat of his fingers. Lord, I was in trouble but good. "Gonna be one hell of a bruise." He looked me over. "But I suppose you'll live," he said.

"So, is this your thing—sneaking up on women in the flower section of Home Depot? Am I going to have to drive across town to Lowe's or do you frequent their garden department, too? How 'bout Walmart?" I continued, walking backward out of his reach.

"Well, ma'am. Not until this moment have I considered garden departments a good place to meet women, but maybe I'll take it up. Leave the bars and online dating and god-awful fix-ups my brother's wife keeps putting me through behind. Load up my cart with all sorts of burly man things like this tiller here and chicken wire and lie in wait for some good-looking woman to close her eyes." He puckered his lips in a smirk and raised his eyebrows, daring me to say who-knows-what. But I found myself unable to rattle off a quick comeback as I normally would, so I stood there nursing my elbow and looking at him like I might punch him any second.

"Can I buy you a Coke and a hot dog?" he asked. "We can push our carts over here to the side. I'll tell the lady up front we're coming back. Please," he said. "Let me make it up to you."

"Fine," I said. "But it better be a damn good dog. And they better have barbecue chips." I followed him like I'd been following him my whole life. My legs equally long. Our strides matched. I wanted to slip my fingers through his belt loops. By the time we made it across the parking lot to the wiener cart, sweat ran down my back, and for a second I felt insecure, but the high was supposed to be in the midnineties so there wasn't a thing either one of us could do. The wet stripe above his stomach stretched by the minute. They had glass-bottle Cokes, and as soon as he handed me one, I held it to my neck like I'd done a thousand times before, but I could see the effect it had on him when he dropped his change, so I took a swig and held it at my side, trying not to do anything else to encourage him so quickly.

"Your dog, ma'am. They're fresh out of barbecue, I'm afraid. It'll have to be plain or sour cream and onion." A bead of sweat ran down his neck.

"Which are you having?" This was not going to be easy.

"Sour cream and onion, of course." He took two bags from the basket on the counter and motioned to a crepe myrtle over at the edge of the parking lot with a little patch of grass. I nodded. I took a whole bunch of extra paper towels from the roll and balanced my food as best I could. Lucky for me he carried my chips. He sat on the curb and crossed his ankles, placing his lunch beside him. "Here," he said, reaching up. "Hand me yours until you get situated."

I didn't quite know what to do with myself, so I sat, pulled my shorts down a little so they didn't hike up too much, and crossed my ankles the same as he had. When I twisted around to crack my back, I didn't even notice the big breath I let out. Being comfortable with someone I'd just met was unheard of for me, but his stature and easy manner was a balm to my high-strung constitution. To hell with not encouraging him. It'd been a long time since I'd met someone as sweet as him. Since I'd met someone who was even interested.

"Sounds like a meal will do you good. The heat and all."

"It's hard to remember to feed yourself when it gets this blasted hot. And you'll faint sure as Christmas if you don't." I took a bite, a glop of mustard and ketchup falling in the grass next to my leg. "Oops."

He dribbled when he took a bite, too.

"Who are you?" I asked. "What kind of man startles a woman with her eyes closed and then goes and buys her a hot dog for goodness' sake? And at Home Depot, no less. I'm not convinced you aren't some hardware store creep."

"My name's Beau. I bought a house down on Flamingo. I come here to hunt for cheap ways to fix up the place so I can sell it for more than I paid for it."

"Down where they're tearing all the old houses down and building McMansions? Tell me you're not Mr. McMansion," I said, crunching up the hot dog wrapper. But I could tell he wasn't. The Mr. McMansions of the world didn't wear work boots splattered in paint or have hair so sun-bleached. Nor did they have big knuckles and the kind of calluses you'd remember when his hands ran down your back. This man could build things. Whole worlds even.

"No, I'm renovating. But I don't want to alter the integrity of the place. It has the original windows. I like the way the world looks from behind the bubbled glass."

"Bubbled glass, huh?" I wiped a last bit of ketchup off his chin. "I'm Layla."

"Like the Clapton song."

"Exactly," I said. "Best not to forget it. But I should say something that's finally come to me now that I'm over the shock of a strange, green-eyed man whispering in my ear. And now the hunger and heat in my brain's calmed down some. You were saying how it's too late to plant hyacinth to enjoy this year, but thing is, I know all about hyacinth, I do. I bet I know more than you. And I was thinking on my Mama is why I stopped next to them. The way she told it, the flowers are native to Anatolia—modern Turkey and all along the Eastern Mediterranean Sea. I like to think about that. The ancestry of little things. She used to say they grew from the blood of a boy Apollo didn't mean to kill. Imagine that. An oops of a manslaughter and because the god who did it feels rotten about it, you get a flower for eternity. I don't know. It's just—there's a lot more to those flowers than you could tell from me closing my eyes and breathing them in. Who are you to assume I don't know?"

"Layla, indeed," he said, standing.

I wiped my face and hands one more time, but the mustard had worked its way under my fingernails. "I need to go wash my hands," I said, showing him the yellow lines.

"Go on, then. I'll meet you in the flowers."

He headed back to the garden department and I took the main entrance in to clean up. Halfway to the door, the wind shifted and hit me with the smell of a hard rain coming. Sure enough, the whirligigs, pinwheels, and flags started whipping and twirling by the time I got to the door. The sky darkened at my back. Storms were always worse when they came from the southwest. It was like every now and then the Gulf took a big-ass breath and blew everything it had our way to prove we weren't any more solid on higher ground.

In the bathroom, the automatic faucets kept turning off. No matter how much foam I lathered, there wasn't enough water pressure to get the mustard out, so I stuck my hands under the industrial-strength dryer and watched my skin ripple, wondering if my hands would look like that in a few decades. Most likely not, as both Mama and Mee-Maw's hands bruised so much in old age they were perpetually the color of eggplant. What was I fussing over anyway? This man obviously didn't care about a bit of mess. A man like that had to be good.

Beau had already loaded up his cart with ornamental grasses. Pampas for privacy. Feather reed grass for texture and a billow of movement on rainy days like today. Fountain grass for winter interest. Because deer won't eat it. Because he liked the way it looked short and bushy in contrast to the others. Trying to imagine what the different varietals would feel like if I plucked a single stalk of each and brushed them on my cheek, I must've closed my eyes again.

"Where'd you go?" He leaned over and tickled my nose with a piece of feather reed grass. "Back to your grandma's?"

"Stop it. One more move like that and you're gonna get yourself hit," I said. Thunder grumbled. The storm wasn't far off now. "Look, I'm a certain kind of woman and I can tell you right now it's not the kind you can tease. And don't even think about pulling pranks if we get into anything here," I said, realizing I hadn't retrieved my own cart yet.

"Get into anything? Does that mean I have a shot at dinner or a drink?" He pushed his cart toward me.

"So long as we understand each other," I said, crossing my arms and looking over my shoulder at the darkening sky.

"Help me get some Pink Lemonade lantana, white geraniums, and marigolds so I can be on my way, and I might give you my number."

"I can do that," he said, backing away. "I saw the lantana over here. Geraniums and marigolds are out front."

"Let me go get my cart," I said, and before I turned, "don't do it again."

Scratching the scruff on his chin, he said, "Yes, ma'am."

On our first date, he took me to the house on Flamingo. I'd primped for hours before he picked me up. I expected a chichi dinner, at least. Now I know better than to have expectations about how a woman should be wooed proper, but back then I was still hoping all the shit I'd seen in movies would hold up somehow. It had for Dee, minus the sister she threw over. But then what did that matter when it was fate? Anyhow, I was more concerned with my makeup and hair falling victim to the humidity than anything. The house of his didn't look like anything much. All his talk about integrity and he'd gutted everything except a few bedroom walls and his precious windows. The place where the sink would go had dripped a puddle on the plywood subfloor. He'd brought a picnic for us, and as much as I could tell he wanted to call one of his subcontractors to yell about the mess, he took a deep breath and led me out the French doors to the patio.

A lady had loved this space.

She'd arranged slate in a circle with a path leading up to the back steps. Though they were overgrown now, the rose-bushes on either side of the walkway had been well-tended once. A white Knock Out bloomed quicker than the rest with a few buds opening. A mint-green glider and a trellis crowned the center of the patio. In the middle of the glider, a basket, and on top, a purple hyacinth in a vase.

After my initial skepticism, I had to admit the man knew how to date. We talked about Charlie and Dee. How Los Angeles might not be good for her. Our childhood was dark enough, but no, I didn't want to get into our traumas yet. I wanted to live in the flowers. In the haze. In the sway of weeping willows. See what he saw behind bubble glass. Drink sugary pink wine. Get it on in the back of his truck under a glittering sky. You can't blame a girl for getting married so quickly. If we'd met any time but late spring, I don't know if I'd have taken to him with such ease.

After the wedding, we moved into the house on Flamingo. It wasn't as finished as I'd hoped it would be. Beau and his buddy Gene had worked the whole week to get the cabinets installed, but we had no countertops. I would come in from the grocery store with bread, peanut butter and jam, or salted ham, and plop the stuff that didn't have to be refrigerated right in the openings where the stone should be. Beau was waiting on the perfect piece of granite. He'd describe his vision of the finished kitchen to me while tracing my belly button, and, if I'm honest, I should have paid more attention to how much he talked and how little got done. I tried not to think about the grit between my toes because the whole place still needed floors. Even the bathrooms didn't have doors. The only doors were the ones leading outside. Lack of privacy, particularly in a marriage, will cause chronic distress, like roiled-up muck at the bottom of the river when the rains keep coming all summer.

I set the bedroom up as best I could, draping tulle over the canopy I'd brought from my place. I painted two end tables I got from the unfinished furniture shop downtown. Mint green like the glider. I placed ten taper candles in iron holders on the mantel. The fireplace hadn't worked in years, but Beau had framed a piece of stained glass and fastened it to the brick and painted the trim white. The bedroom looked good. But that was me and Beau in the beginning. The bedroom always looked good.

A few months after we moved in, Beau and Gene went in on another flip house at the riverfront. After a year, our house remained identical to the day we moved in. We'd browse all the junk shops and hardware stores for fifty miles, but we never bought anything. The truth was he'd spent all my inheritance and any money he had on the new place. He thought he was keeping our money troubles hidden. So he'd make a show of haggling. Of course it wouldn't go well, and Beau would turn stingy and mean, walking off, leaving me to smooth things over half the time. At an artists' colony outside Asheville, a short woman with asymmetrical hair and a pentagram tattoo in the center of her chest was so off-put by Beau's energy when he wanted to buy a truck bed repurposed into a bench for the front hall, she asked us to leave after watching us for only a few short minutes. Beau knocked over a whole table of blown glass ornaments on the way out.

"Let me help you clean up," I said. "I'm so sorry."

"You have no cause to apologize to me, ma'am. I'm afraid it's you that needs help cleaning up. I don't know how to say this except to come straight out with it."

"Say what you need to say," I said, trying to memorize the shape of the shattered glass.

"When I look at him, I see black tar where his teeth should be," she said as she turned her back on me, kneeling to sweep up the mess. "Go," she said. "He won't be happy if you keep him waiting."

I barely had the car door closed when he peeled out, flinging gravel everywhere without a second thought toward the family walking by with two children and a golden retriever panting at their side. By the time we got home, he behaved as if the whole incident had never happened. He opened the door for me and led me out of the car and into the house. Once again, we came home empty-handed.

"Baby," he said. "Can't you see it? The kitchen shiny with granite and crystal. Salvaged brass. Just as shiny as you. That's what I want."

Not wanting to break his mood, I replied as I had a thousand times before: "It sounds like a dream." My feet hurt from walking in flats on gravel so I swapped my shoes for the slippers I kept by the front door and turned to go upstairs.

"You going to lie down?" he asked.

"Yes, the heat and all that walking. I'm exhausted."

"Maybe I'll join you."

"I thought you were meeting up with Gene," I said, running my hand along the guardrail—one of the few projects he'd finished. The wood grain's luster wasn't lost on me. "This morning you were going on about it."

"We could get some work done, if you're okay with it," he said, kissing my hand.

"Have fun," I said.

And so I had the evening to myself. When I woke the first time, the sun had already set and the boatlike motion of my dreams had left me feeling ill. I sat up so I could rub my arches for a spell and get a glass of ice water, but before I could get downstairs, Beau turned up the drive and headlights blinded me for longer than they should've. He took his time getting out of the car. A song I could've recognized if it had been a bit louder made my heart hurt. But it didn't take much for my heart to hurt these days. I settled for sink water and went back to bed.

Eventually, Beau came to bed. "I'm home," he said. "You awake?"

"No."

He smelled like campfire, cheap whiskey, and faintly of cinnamon. His hand on my hip. A long silence passed. Then, his foot slid up my calf. A signal I knew well, but I grew weary with the house. It consumed him. I rolled away from his foot, squinching up my pillow between my legs. My back hadn't been right since we moved in. He grew frustrated by my lack of reciprocation and let his foot drop. His hand stayed still. Evening light hit the stained glass, washing the plywood with shades of blue and green, bringing it to life.

"I don't know anymore, Beau. Do you even know what you're doing with this place?"

My breath quickened.

He shoved me with the same force he'd tossed the display table. Though I caught myself on the edge of the bed, my body knew bruises were already forming. Blood under skin.

"I don't know why I thought a redneck bitch like you would understand," he said. "I'm sleeping downstairs."

"On what?"

"Blankets."

"I'm sorry," I said, reaching for him as he put a pillow under each arm.

When Daddy died, it was sudden. There was no lengthy illness. No anticipatory grief or praying for his suffering to end. There was a last day like any other. He came home from the fields, took his boots off, ate a turkey TV dinner Mama fixed for him, and died in his easy chair sometime in the night, Bob Ross painting in the background. The coroner said it must've been a stroke or a heart attack since the tray was on the floor and his can of Pepsi spilled on his pants. I had a feeling they lied about the Pepsi. No one wants to tell a wife and a daughter that the man they knew and loved peed himself as he died. But it happens. It's almost never peaceful or pretty. Years ago, Daddy found his sister Jo in her den—ass to the sky and purple-faced—with her two little dogs running in circles around her, yapping at him. They were hungry and scared and covered in their own filth. He and his sisters had argued about what to do for services, what to do with the remains, who got what. I guess that's another reason Daddy put all his wishes on paper.

In the night, I woke crampy and bleeding. Without turning on any lights, I cleaned myself, changed my gown, and stripped the sheets. It had been storming all night and finally seemed to be letting up, so I sprayed the stains, dropped them in the washer, and wrote myself a note to wash them after breakfast. The streetlight shone through the glass on the back door, making it glow, making it seem cool and clean and born of a different world, so I walked over and turned the knob as quietly as I could, but old houses speak. The patio was still my favorite part of the house—the best part of me and Beau. It had quit raining but steam rose from the ground and the frogs had started talking again. A quiet meep came from a nest in the top corner of the trellis. For weeks, I'd waited for them to hatch and watched them long enough to see their down come in. When I sat on the glider, water soaked through my gown, so I went ahead and leaned back, kicking off my slippers and pushing the ground with my bare feet. If only Beau weren't under so much pressure. If only he hadn't bought that second house. His beeper and phone went off constantly. If we had floors, maybe I wouldn't be so wounded. Linoleum. Bamboo. Heart of pine. Plush carpet. Ceramic tile. Smooth and cool. Textured and warm. Soft. Clean. The scent of Murphy Oil Soap.

I almost fell asleep again out in the wet haze. But the mist and steam turned back into rain, so I headed for cover. When I stepped up on the back steps, I turned back to look at the glider one more time. The spot where I'd lain now pooling water. The dying scuppernong vines on the trellis. As I looked closer, an unnatural black silhouette jutted up out of the bird's nest. I ran over, my feet slapping against the wet slate. A snake with a marked bulge in its belly had enveloped the nest. When the truth of what I saw hit me, I screamed and fell to my knees.

Within seconds, Beau ran toward me in his shorts with an ax in his hand. "Baby? What? What is it?"

"Snake. Snake got the birds," I said, pointing.

Beau looked at me confused and started to turn, but when he couldn't get me up off the ground, when he couldn't stop my sobbing with his touch, he pulled the thing down by its tail. It landed with a thud. Before I knew it, he'd hacked the poor snake's head off. The slate darkened. My green-eyed, long-lashed husband tossed the head in the yard and asked me if I was happy now. "It's dead," he said, pushing his hair back, leaving a streak of blood on his forehead. "Don't that make you happy at least?" When I kept crying, he picked up the carcass and pulled out three birds and dropped them on my lap. "There," he said. "Now it's over. Bury them and clean yourself up."

I pulled my gown up, making a hammock for them, wondering where their parents were, if they'd watched, or if they were used to that sort of thing. Maybe nature was simply nature and the birds felt nothing and would start building a new nest at first light after they fed themselves, but I would never believe such a thing, so I dug in the wet earth with my hands until I thought I had a hole big enough for all three of them next to the white Knock Out roses. I didn't want them to be lonely. When I was satisfied with the grave, I placed them on the grass above—still soft, still whole—pulled my gown over my head, put them in the middle of it at the waist ribbon, and folded the garment as small as I could, laying them to rest as the rain let up. When I finished singing "Amazing Grace" for the birds, I put the snake carcass around my neck and went off to search for its discarded head.

DEADHEADING

Every morning, Layla drank her coffee on the porch of her little shotgun house up in the hills, an hour outside of nowhere, the music of the land all she could hear save for an occasional plane on its way to Asheville. Rituals like two cups of coffee outdoors in her nubby lounge pants before the day's work began helped set her mind right. Get some distance from her shit marriage. Like replacing a blood-stained sheet for one freshly laundered. Volatile. Volatile was what she told the police when they came looking for Beau after he disappeared. Asking questions Layla couldn't answer. The man never told Layla anything about his goings-on. All she could see was his descent. The panicked way he stomped around the house. The staggering weight he lost in a few short months. She'd spent the better part of two years trying to make sense of it. And so each morning she sipped from the same chipped "Seize The Day Then Go Back To Bed" mug her sister had given her years ago. Before their mama died, before they'd married the wrong men, when they still spent half their nights at home. Dee had left the thing on the kitchen counter with a Hershey's bar and a note: "Happy Birthday, Bitch." Easy joy was Layla's focus these days.

Since she moved, Layla had stopped getting her hair cut, and the way it brushed against her elbows when she rocked made her skin prickle. She relished coffee with chicory. Chocolate pound cake for breakfast from her mama's recipe taped to the mini-fridge. After the collapse of her marriage, easy was all she could hope for. The thought of any romantic attachment made her hands tremble. Hands big-knuckled and strong from staking tomatoes and kneading bread. Flour and earth and green forever caked in her nails. Instead of a second marriage, she knew her future lay in grains, in the tensile strength of plants, in hanging on to the fibrous textures of the flora she'd immersed herself in. Deadheading flowers and pounding dough and pulling weeds.

She hadn't minded too much about Beau's mysterious departure. After the incident with the snake and all, she was relieved at how quickly her marriage had ceased to be. It could have been uglier, but when she said those words out loud, folks would look at her sideways and say things like, "Layla, honey, you can't mean that. The man up and vanished and everybody knows what come of him. He was your husband." She'd always nod and say, "Yes, yes of course. I didn't mean it that way. My poor angel." But most folks didn't know about the incident or how he'd changed since they married. They didn't know she was lucky things went the way they did or she might be the one disappeared into nothing like so many women before her. Folks hadn't seen the blood smear on his forehead, still wet, as he ate a bowl of cereal. Folks hadn't seen the way he hacked off that snake's head and pulled out those bird babies. Or how he tossed them in her lap. Two years later, she still couldn't reconcile the man she'd married to the man at her kitchen table that morning. After they found his car stripped at the junkyard, Layla had no trouble turning the house they'd lived in together over to the men who come for it—three brothers—each one more leathered than the next, with baseball bats resting on their shoulders. The light that day was July bright and blinding. No part of anyone, least of all Layla or the backs of her knees, was dry. The biggest fella smacked a mosquito on his neck, pulled a handkerchief from his back pocket, and wiped his whole face, including the corners of his mouth.

"Lady, we need a word," he said, folding the handkerchief and placing it back in his pocket.

"The polite thing to do would be to introduce yourselves," she said, shielding her eyes with her hand. "I don't believe I've met any of y'all before." Layla wore her daisy housedress, the one she mooned over and bought because yes, the print was her favorite flower, but mostly because it had pockets. A dress with pockets is a reason to celebrate on its own, but as she slid her right hand down to grip the revolver she was hiding, she congratulated herself again for a fine dress purchase. "Besides, I knew you needed a word the minute you turned up my street. I don't know where Beau's at, if that's what you're after."

"No, ma'am. It ain't that. And my name's Waylon and these are my brothers, if you want to know." The other two stood mute, rolling their bats on their shoulders. "I hate you're mixed up in your husband's affairs, but I can't change the facts and the fact is this house here belongs to us now."

Layla took a few steps closer to the brothers. The air was stagnant and even the tall grass seemed to wince under the heat. She held tight to the gun, running her thumb over the handle. The men straightened their backs and the mute brothers glanced from Layla to Waylon and back again. She looked over her shoulder at the house, took a deep breath, and sighed. "I never wanted this place anyway. As far as I can see, Beau got what was coming to him, and the fact that he got it before he could do me any more harm than he did is a damn miracle." She let go of the gun and reached her hand out to Waylon. "Give me some time to gather my things," she said, looking hard into the man's gray eyes. He could've been attractive if he'd been there under different circumstances.

"I'm not sure it's a good idea to let you," he said, scanning the house and yard again.

"You'll get no trouble from me. Take it," she said. "From the moment I crossed the threshold, my life's been shit."

The brothers lowered their bats. The smallest one said,

"We're awful sorry for coming here like this, but honey, let me tell you, your man was some nasty piece of work." His brows pinched and he took half a step forward before changing his mind, and he and the other quiet one returned to the beater they come in.

"We'll give you a week to collect your things," Waylon said. "That's about the best we can do. Do the smart thing, ma'am. I don't want to hurt someone who looks so much like my mama."

A cluster of clouds rolled in front of the sun and a breeze kicked up and swallowed itself again before anyone had a chance to be grateful. "I'll be out by Friday," she said, waving goodbye with one hand and wrapping her waist with the other, like she was saying farewell to someone dear, the pain of which burrowed into her belly.

She kept her word. Layla took two days to gather a few copper planters that had belonged to her mother, her daddy's mantel clock, and though she'd long since distanced herself from it, his beloved, marked-up King James. Pulling clothes out of her closet, she realized she didn't need half of what she had. She dropped an armful of dresses on the floor and walked out with one suitcase and two boxes. Objects take on energy and she had no wish to carry it with her.

Layla loved the calmer air up in the woods. The knock of a woodpecker. His flash of red high in the pecan tree. A stack of romance novels in the corner she'd bought from the used bookstore up in Hendersonville. She liked to pick at the flaking paper on them and preferred tales written in the seventies because the newer ones, with all those bone-headed women who thought they wanted to be submissives, made her ill. They had no idea. Layla put her feet up on the railing, took a last swig from her mug, and put it down beside her. Next door, Adelaide and the twins worked all morning. Feeding the last of her hens, chopping wood for the stove. The girls ran loose under the sheets on the line. Layla and Adelaide had only spoken these past few years out of necessity. Sharing garden yields. Loaning her the truck once a month when she went into town for supplies. Pulling a tarp over the storm-damaged chicken coop. Layla wanted to ask Adelaide a million times how she'd come to live up there, about the girls' daddy, but she knew better. Whatever the details, it was trauma of one form or another. Women see what men filter. It's in the gait, in the slope of the shoulders, in the purple-rimmed eyes. Watching the sheets billow made Layla wonder where Adelaide did the washing, how she got the white so blasted white it like to blind her. All Layla had was an old brown machine on the back stoop, and though she missed the softness a dryer added, she'd learned to enjoy the smell of the outdoors on her clothes. A hint of woodsmoke, wildflower, or pine, depending on the season. She'd given up trying to get anything white herself. But something was off that morning. There was a fever to

Adelaide's manner she'd not observed before. She scrubbed her porch with a bucket of soap and water like she was trying to take the paint off. She'd sit up every now and then, wipe her face with her sleeve, and shove the brush back in the water with her other hand. By the time she finished, she was wet from knee to chest. When she was done, she carried the bucket over to the side of the house like she was about to do the same thing with the windows. But when she caught sight of the girls running wild, she pulled a switch off an overgrown rosebush and swatted them into the house. The woodpecker stopped knocking away at the pecan tree and all grew quiet. The sheets flapped hard in the wind. Plumes rising from the chimney eventually petered out.

In the quiet, Layla fell asleep with the sun warming her face and a book open in her lap. She often dreamed of being overtaken by kudzu. It was hell to kill and when she'd cut the root of one part, the other grew stronger and faster. Snakes burrowed in it. Copperheads and black snakes, rat and eastern rattlers. She never paid snakes any mind before the incident, but now she could hardly sleep without them making an appearance. Dreams so vivid she could still hear them moving through the foliage once she woke. A pointy-headed copperhead was winding up her leg when a gunshot rang out, waking her with a jerk. Her feet fell off the railing, still dead numb from how she'd propped them.

The forest turned silent. Every living creature seemed to hold its breath.

And then—twigs broke, leaves shushed, and birds took flight when little feet hit the ground with the hot momentum that could only be panic. In an instant, one of the girls came barreling through Layla's yard, heading straight for the pond. Her braids, undone, fell in her eyes. Poor child had welts from knee to ankle and her face—gray as a dove's wing. By the time she reached the edge of Layla's property, she tripped, hitting the ground with a yelp. The girl looked back over her shoulder, her chin scraped and bleeding, and for a few short breaths, she hesitated. The pistol she carried had fallen out of her pocket in the process, but the girl hadn't noticed. It lay glinting under a tree root as she righted herself and resumed running until she reached the water. Layla stood, paralyzed, as Adelaide dragged her other daughter by one braid, following the same path toward the pond.

Layla hollered for her to turn the girl loose, but Adelaide never looked up, and without stopping, she leaned down for the pistol, tucking it in her waistband; the child had quit kicking at that point and let herself go limp. "Wait, wait!" Layla screamed. "Leave those babies alone."

She had done so much nothing in her life.

It took Layla a few moments. She watched from another galaxy, another solar system, some other blue planet with a different gravity. A space where breaths were years. People wonder how anyone can stand by while abuse happens. Those people have never been abused. They've never known fight or flight or how the second someone lays their hands on you in violence, everything's changed. How the mind wants to make it your fault. One of the girls screamed again and the sound jerked Layla's ass in gear. For the first time in months, she made a phone call. "Up at Beulah Church Road, the pond end," she said. "My neighbor. She's hurting her babies." Then, she dropped the phone, threw on her garden clogs, and ran after them.

When Layla first moved in, she couldn't sleep. The hard truth was she missed Beau despite everything. The shame spiral that came when she thought of him, his heavy legs draped over hers, left her straining to hear animal sounds in the night, trying to figure out who crossed in the dark. Once, she heard a doe and two fawns. Hefty, cracking steps followed by soft, unsteady ones.

She'd tried therapy shortly after Beau disappeared, told Wanda, the sweet old gal, all about the change in him after they'd married. How he called her a redneck piece of shit for leaning out the front door to call him in for dinner. How he called her trash all the time. But how she tried to fight his moods with plates piled high with love. Only love can crisp chicken skin like that. "He'd been such a sweet potato," she said. "And his eyes. How can someone with the ocean in his eyes turn so cold?" She neglected to tell her they'd said their vows less than two months after they met. Layla couldn't speak truth to her no matter how soothing the woman's voice or how sleepy the lavender oil made the room. She never could make eye contact, opting instead to gaze at the light of the diffuser moving from cool blue to violet to green.

"What do you know about his past?" Wanda had asked, making a note on her pad.

Layla crossed her arms over her chest and picked a scab on her shoulder. The wallpaper was gaudy. Black swirls, gold leaves, and obnoxious dinner plate mums. "You know," she said, "in real life, those flowers wouldn't hold their own weight. They'd have to be staked. Who wants to go to all that trouble for something that blooms for half a minute only to fall over on itself?"

"Interesting that you'd put it that way."

"I don't like the wallpaper. That's all," she said, pulling the last of the scab off, then realizing Wanda watched her do this. "Sorry," Layla said.

"No need to apologize."

Layla pulled a tissue from the box on the coffee table, wrapped the scab up, and put it in her pocket. "I don't know much about Beau's past. I suppose I married him out of loneliness and what seemed like his sweet nature. In the beginning, he cradled me when I hurt myself. My instincts are shit."

"Deception doesn't mean there weren't good moments. Some of what you felt was true. Maybe some of what he showed you was true, too," she said.

Wanda talked a lot about Layla's perception of the world. Threw words around about disordered thinking and splitting and coping mechanisms for the trauma she'd endured. The tragedy of her experience was not her identity. If she focused on the positive moments that came after, how it's made her a stronger woman than she thinks, she could build a new life out of that, find new love, maybe still have children. But Layla knew after she'd seen Beau pull baby birds out of that snake's belly, motherhood was off the table. She quit seeing Wanda after a month. It was only a few days later those men come for the house and she packed her shit for a quieter life. But the quiet had enveloped her more than she thought it would, and when her legs began to cramp in the night, she found herself walking the woods when the moon shone brightly enough. She smoked cigarette after cigarette on the overgrown shore of the pond. From time to time, an owl would call out, but no mate ever answered. Layla may have bloodied her feet on warm nights, but the walking wounds made her feel part of the great conversation, a warrior of the land that remade her.

Layla hadn't gotten more than a few feet from her porch

before she lost her shoes. Her feet could take it. Adelaide had reached the pond's shoreline, the girl still in tow. The twin who made it to the water was pulling herself up on an outcrop on the other side. As she turned to face her mother, sister, and Layla, she flung her wet hair back. She stood glaring, wondering what Adelaide would do next. All at once, she fell to the ground, rummaging in her pockets, and when she realized the gun was gone, her head dropped and she placed both palms on the boulder that held her.

Adelaide yelled, "I got the gun safe right here. Come on back now, and we'll see what can be done." She pulled the pistol from her waistband and lowered it to her side, clicking the safety off as she did, but the way she held the gun was off. Her dominant hand was still wrapped in twelve inches' worth of her daughter's hair and if she had any hope of shooting proper, Adelaide would need to switch hands.

A silk wind blew across the pond, rippling the water and sending orange-tipped leaves fluttering to the ground. Pecans dropped. Layla slowed her pace and took more care with where she placed her feet, remembering the delicate sound of fawns. She stepped behind an ancient pine, trying to find her breath. Her feet were numb, but her chest stung with every inhalation. In the stillness, a salamander crawled over her toes, pausing momentarily to look side to side before it returned to the safety of leaf cover. Layla pulled her hair back into a low bun with the rubber band she kept around her wrist, trying to calculate her move. The whole fever of her marriage and its carnage showed in her cheeks and the veins at her temples. The world pounded and flushed.

While she was still on her knees, the girl across the pond lifted her head and looked at her mother, her body beginning to stiffen. The child was no fawn. She pulled her wet dress over her head and hardened her jaw, shoulders, and the rest of her body until she seemed a natural predator scanning the ground below. The girl rose. Rose into her own kind of animal, baby-skinned but sister-fierce and fearless.

"I said get your ass back here. If you do right, maybe I'll let you live. What you done. You ought to be ashamed. But come back and do right, and we'll see."

"Let her go," the child screamed, before diving back into the water. The sound of the splash was all it took for her sister to begin fighting again, biting at their mother's ankle and trying with all her might to kick her knees out from under her. With little effort, Adelaide dodged her kicks, never letting go of her hair in the process. She was pulling her scalp so hard it looked like it would come clean off, but the girl gathered her strength, grabbed hold of her own hair with one hand, and swung with the other, managing to get one good hit in right in her mother's sternum. Out of instinct, her mother's hands went to her chest. The girl was free, if only for a moment. When Adelaide looked back to the pond, her other daughter had almost reached the bank, her breaststroke furious.

Layla stepped out from behind the tree, motioning for the girl to come to her as she approached, but as she got close enough to grab her, Adelaide swung around and hit the child with the gun square across the forehead. The girl stumbled backward, a white gash visible for a second before the blood came. Adelaide and Layla made eye contact, but they could see the girl in the periphery convulsing on the ground, stirring an ants' nest she fell on. The women circled each other like boxers might, but the movement was so careful and slow.

"Mind your business, Layla."

"I can't sit idle on this one, Adelaide. Those are your children," Layla said, noticing the gun's steadiness in her hand now. "I done sat by for too much of my life."

"You don't have any idea what it's like," she said, stopping next to her daughter, who'd finally stilled. A braid lay across her face, catching blood. "Day in and day out. I try to teach them right. To protect them. But they gon' be wrong, gon' do wrong, no matter."

"Adelaide, these are your children. Look what you've done to your daughter," Layla said, finally looking directly at the child. Ants had swarmed her arms and neck, but the girl hadn't budged. "I won't let you hurt them further."

Adelaide pointed the gun at the girl on the ground without a sound but turned again to figure out her other daughter's position. She was no longer in the water. "Come out, August. I can smell your stink." She squinted and craned, but couldn't make her out. Layla knew she was coming up behind her mother—naked save for her faded pink underwear—but tried not to show any changes on her face. Layla kept her lips still when August scooped up the biggest rock she could find. Relaxed her cheeks when she saw the scars on the girl's chest. Squelched her flaring nostrils when she realized how much she'd failed to notice before now. As Layla focused her attention on the unconscious sister for fear of giving August away, she became increasingly worried for June's life. Her breaths per minute slowed.

"Adelaide, June needs a doctor," she said. "She's like to die from her wound. Let me at least see to her."

"Stay where you're at, Layla. Don't move. Not even one of your God-awful-looking man toes." She turned sideways so she could get a better view of her surroundings. "I hear you August. The second I see you, child, one of you is getting a bullet. I never should have had you girls. I never should have kept you. Your father said to go see somebody about it, get rid of it, you all. Damn if he wasn't right."

Layla had leaned down to brush the ants off June's legs when August emerged again. She was still lake-clean, but you could see the lashes on her thighs were fresh. In moments that move so fast, when you'd think the mind would trim the fat of everyday thoughts, Layla remembered that first hot dog she ate with Beau. How a perfect few minutes seemed to suck the joy out of the rest of her life. Idleness. Blood. Scars and bruises and twin girls beaten wild when she'd never have a child of her own. And as August's arms raised up executioner silent, Layla shoved Adelaide to the ground. August looked down, ready to launch anyway, but Layla picked up the gun, cocked it, and shot, rubbing the handle for a second before sliding it in the back of her pants. August still had her arms raised, but now her glare shifted to Layla.

"It's over, honey."

"But," she breathed, wildebeest and lioness.

"I know. You don't have to say it. Come on, doll, and put the rock down. It's time to see to your sister."

August placed the rock next to June and sat down. She looked her sister over, moved the braid out of her face, noticing the shift in the shade of her lips. She licked her hand and tried to wipe some of the blood off her cheek, but her sister's breath was gone. Layla felt for a pulse and finding none, sat up on her knees and continued brushing the ants off the child's legs. They were the only two mourners June would have.

Eventually, Layla convinced August to come with her to her house to get cleaned up, where she washed her long hair in the kitchen sink and sent her to the tub to clean herself the rest of the way. When she came out, she wore the clothes Layla had picked out for her, a simple blue T-shirt and some tie-string plaid bottoms. Of course the clothes swallowed the girl, but at least she looked human again, all tender girl bone and soft skin. "Come here, love, and I'll comb the knots out of your hair." August said nothing but joined her on the sofa, sitting with her back to Layla. If there was anything Layla knew, it was how to comb long hair without hurting. It's best to gather it in one hand at the ends and brush a few inches at a time, slowly making your way up to the crown. It took an hour to get the tangles out.

August looked at Layla with an expression of gratitude, soft eyebrows and sighs at the corners. "I wish I could comb June's hair," she said, looking at the floor.

"Look at me, August," Layla said, turning her chin with her hand. "If that's what you truly want, if it's something you'll regret the rest of your life if you don't, we can do it. We can do it tomorrow before we bury her. I'll prepare everything."

"But the blood," she said.

"We can take a bucket of warm water and the same strawberry shampoo I used on you. If you want. But child, can I say something?"

"Yes, ma'am."

"Whatever it is your mother said y'all done wrong can't have been bad enough to deserve all this. You need to hear those words and let them sink in for real or this day won't be the last of something terrible, but the beginning of everything worse."

August cried a little but wiped her face and sat silent and staring at the door. The hens had settled down for the night and a slow rain began to patter on the tin roof. The girl looked more tired than any grown woman Layla had ever seen. "Go on and go to sleep, if you can. You take my bed and I'll sleep in here on the couch."

The child said okay and wandered to the bedroom, touching the wall every few feet. After an hour, Layla looked in to see how she was doing. August had pulled the sheet up over her head, but Layla could tell she was asleep by the depth of her breaths and, though they were muffled, the tiny whimpers of a dreaming girl.

She had done so much nothing before now.

ACKNOWLEDGMENTS

The author wishes to thank the following publications in which some of these pieces first appeared:

Best Microfiction 2019: "Bone Words"; *Cheap Pop*: "A Five-Pointed Failed Paper Love Weapon"; *Cotton Xenomorph*: "For A Blaze of Sight"; *Elke: A Little Journal*: "Gwen of All Gwens"; *Hot Metal Bridge*: "A Little Arrhythmic Blip"; *Jellyfish Review*: "Earth Eating As Suppression"; *Little Patuxent Review*: "Fly the Car to Mars"; *Longleaf Review*: "Bone Words"; *Menacing Hedge*: "Still Soft, Still Whole"; *Noble/Gas Qtrly*: "Like Air, or Bread, or Hard Apple Candy"; *Storychord*: "The Gopher in Rae's Chest"; *Synaesthesia Magazine*: "The Best Kind of Light"; *This Zine Will Change Your Life*: "Tomorrow or Tomorrow" (as "Turbulent Like May, Wet Like June"); and *Wigleaf*: "Lake Harwell, South Carolina."

This book is many years in the making, and I'm not sure I would have survived the grief and trauma without the act of creating this thing you now hold in your hands. Thank you to Jim and Aubrie for your love and support. Thank you to Ben for putting up with me over the years and taking care of the critters when I went off to write alone in the woods. I love you. Thank you to editors Georgia Bellas and Annie Frazier, who made this book infinitely better. A huge thank you to Kate Gale, Elizabeth Bradfield for selecting my manuscript, and the whole team at Red Hen Press for all your beautiful work and unyielding kindness. Thank you to Steph Post, Robert James Russell, Jared Yates Sexton, and Leesa Cross-Smith for your time and generosity in writing blurbs. Thanks also to Angela Frey, Carrie Renegar, Kathy Fish, Sherrie Flick, Troy Palmer, Alvin Park, Kris Bernard, Lee Krecklow, Jeff Pfaller, Nancy Stohlman, Chloe Clark, Cathy Ulrich, Maureen Langloss, and Jayne Martin for your many kindnesses. I am also grateful to the folks at Sundress Academy for the Arts, C3 Lab, and Charlotte Lit for the space to create. And finally, a lifetime of gratitude to my mom and brother for always encouraging art making of all kinds.

BIOGRAPHICAL NOTE

Beth Gilstrap is the author of *I Am Barbarella* (2015) from Twelve Winters Press. Her work has been selected as Longform.org's "Fiction Pick of the Week" and chosen by Dan Chaon for inclusion in the *Best Microfiction Anthology 2019*. She holds an MFA from Chatham University. Her stories, essays, and hybrids have appeared in *Ninth Letter*, the *Minnesota Review*, *Denver Quarterly*, *Gulf Stream Lit*, and *Wigleaf*, among others. Born and raised in the Charlotte area, she has recently relocated to Louisville.